DEATH COMES A-CALLIN'!

Rocklin glimpsed the sniper moving along the base of the cliff. He quickly bent down and turned the dead man over, slipping the six-shooter out of its holster. Then he took cover behind some rocks.

The sniper wasn't long in coming. He dismounted, looked down at the body of his victim, and then started going through his pockets. He saw that the dead man's gun was missing, looked around for it, and then stood up, puzzled. There was blood on his hands and he wiped them on his denims and rested his right hand on the gun in his holster. He was still looking around when Rocklin stepped out from behind the rock and said, "Here it is."

Faster than Rocklin had any reason to expect, the sniper's Colt cleared leather in one swift movement . . .

LAST RIDE
TO
ROCKY MESA

JACK AINTRY

ZEBRA BOOKS
KENSINGTON PUBLISHING CORP.

ZEBRA BOOKS

are published by

Kensington Publishing Corp.
475 Park Avenue South
New York, NY 10016

First printing: June, 1989

Printed in the United States of America

One

"You're going to have to make it plainer."

Rocklin leaned back in his chair and glared at Bannister, who made a triangle with some pencils on his desk and didn't answer.

"Well?" Rocklin demanded.

"How much plainer does it need to be?" Bannister asked, not looking up.

Rocklin got up and started for the door.

"I'm not finished," Bannister said quietly.

Rocklin stopped and turned his glare on the man he respected as much as any man he knew, and frequently trusted with his life. "All right," he said. "But remember, we've been through this before. When you start holding back, it means you don't like the smell of the deal. So I repeat. You're going to have to make it plainer. A lot plainer."

Bannister sighed. "Sit down." Rocklin sat and waited. Bannister sighed again. "Did you ever hear of a place called Rathole?"

"I've heard of it. A gang hideout. No one even

approaches it and lives, unless he knows the right signal and someone in the town who'll vouch for him. Are you saying that's where the Heller bunch is hanging out?"

"Yes."

Rocklin leaned back again. Now his face was expressionless. "I want it all."

"Do you know where it is?"

"Roughly."

Bannister nodded. "That's as much as anyone else knows." He rose and pulled down a wall map behind his desk. "All right. Here's Pine Hollow. As I told you, this is where Big Jim Haggard's place is. Up here at about nine thousand feet is Granite Pass. If you leave the trail just before you get to the summit and head northwest, you come to the Rocky Mesa country. There is apparently nothing up there. It's impossible to reach, unless you're a mountaineer, and it's about two and a half miles from east to west, and about twenty miles from north to south. But Rathole is up there somewhere."

"Only fifty square miles."

Bannister glanced at Rocklin, who seldom resorted to sarcasm. "It's not that bad. We know the route they take up. At least we know their starting point."

"And just how do you know that?"

Bannister sat down and turned a level gaze on Rocklin. "Big Jim Haggard questioned a rustler who got a few miles up the trail before he was shot to pieces. He got a few answers out of him before he died."

"When was this?"

"A month ago. He told one of my men at the Cattlemen's Association about it just the other day. The Association wants action."

"Because of a few rustled cattle? No. They never did raid the Slattery gang's hideout in Robber's Roost. They knew it wasn't worth the cost. In human life, that is. What else? Let's have it, Bannister."

"You know about the Gladstone Tunnel fire."

"Who doesn't? It closed the tunnel on the transcontinental railroad for four months."

"The fire was set, just a quarter of a mile inside the east portal. It stopped a train; and the train, and everybody in it, was robbed."

"I knew about the fire and about the robbery, but I didn't know about the connection."

"Not many people do. Three people were killed during the robbery, all of them railroad employees. Six men were killed repairing the tunnel."

"So that's it. And since cross-country tours have become popular with the East Coast upper crust, and very profitable for the railroad . . . Why doesn't the railroad put a half-dozen of their troubleshooters on it? Or twenty? Or thirty?"

"They have."

Silence. Finally, Rocklin said, "I see. And of course the train was carrying mail, so the federal government is involved." He waited for a reply but didn't get one. "And banks have been robbed in, what? One state and two territories? Big losses. I read the papers. So *they* have had special agents working on it, too. They must be stumbling over

7

each other out there." No reply. "And the rustling must be small potatoes compared to the other criminal enterprises." Still no reply. "So why did they bring it to you? I want to know."

Bannister cleared his throat. "There was a conference of, uh, all the parties involved. At the highest level, I am told. They decided to turn it over to us."

"Us?"

"The Association," Bannister said.

"Were any names mentioned?"

"No. There was only one person at the conference who even knows my name. I wasn't there, of course."

Rocklin thought for a minute. "Was there any talk, even a hint, of my existence? I mean that someone like me will be involved? Come on, Bannister, that's the least I need to know. Let's have it."

"Any talk that someone like you would be involved was carefully avoided."

This time the silence stretched as Rocklin thought for much longer than a minute about the implications of Bannister's answers. Then he said, "If I take the job, it will cost you."

"Naturally."

"All right, to begin with, I want all the reports. All of them. From the railroad, from the Pinkertons if they were in on it, from your own men, from anyone else who has had anything to do with this tangle from the very beginning."

"You know I can't do that. In the first place, we wouldn't get all the information. Those outfits

8

would hold out on us, and you know it. And there are things about *my* operation that I can't possibly reveal, and wouldn't do you any good, anyway. Be reasonable, Rocklin.''

"I want everything pertinent you can get your hands on, or I don't take it on. From my point of view, that is not only reasonable but essential. Put pressure on that 'highest level.' It's up to you.''

"But you haven't actually said that you *will* take it on.''

"Of course not. I'll decide when I've digested the reports. That's it, Bannister.''

"What about Big Jim? He's still in town. Will you want to talk to him?

"No. Not now and not ever. For all I know, he's in on it. Have the director of the Association put him off, tell him you're studying the situation, tell him anything. If you want to risk another man, send someone out to string him along and keep him out of the way.

"Get the reports, give me a week or so to study them, and I'll let you know. I'm going home. Wire me in New York.''

"But I may have everything for you in a couple of days.''

"It will wait. There's someone I have to talk to.''

Two

Rocklin read the reports Bannister had gathered and flatly refused to talk about his plans.

Bannister tried to tell him that he had to have something to show the director of the Association, especially in view of the large fee that Rocklin had demanded in advance, but Rocklin was in a take-it-or-leave-it mood. He had not been encouraged by the reports.

"What about a contact point?" Bannister asked.

"There won't be one."

"You expect to be gone two or three months—"

"Maybe four or five."

"—leaving me completely in the dark."

"There's no other way, Bannister, and you know it." Rocklin picked up a stack of papers from Bannister's desk and waved them at him. "Haven't you read these reports?"

"I've read them."

"Well?"

Bannister sighed.

"At least five men have tried to join that bunch of killers—two of them actually had criminal records—and where are they?" He didn't need an answer.

"So you're not going to try that." It was a statement.

"By the way, is there a telegraph office in Pine Hollow? The reports didn't say."

"No, but there's a wire at Fort Hatcher down on the flat, ten miles due east. I'm that close, Rocklin."

"Good enough. How many men can you muster at a moment's notice?"

"I can get a troop of cavalry from any post in the area by lifting the phone."

Rocklin stood up. "If you don't hear from me in four months, I've failed and I'm dead. See you later, Bannister." He went out and shut the door behind him.

Three

Rocklin didn't go through Pine Hollow at all. He got off the train at Russell Junction, twenty miles north of the Hollow, and spent the first day pampering Buck, the sturdy buckskin that he considered indispensable no matter what the job was. It had been a tedious trip for both man and horse—almost two thousand miles and three train changes—and Rocklin was glad to take Buck to the broad mountain meadow below the Junction and let him stretch out and run. He groomed him and fed him oats and scattered fresh straw in his stall at the livery stable; then he set about outfitting for a prospecting trip, a long one.

Russell Junction was a railroad town, the last stop on a major east-west line before the trains headed up toward the Great Divide. There was a switching yard, there was a roundhouse, extra rolling stock, a snowplow. And there was a busy atmosphere of people coming and going. It was a good place to spend a week, talking to strangers about the surrounding country, gossiping in barbershops, hotel restaurants, and saloons. It was the usual casual talk: where the hunting and fishing were best (the locals, as usual, had their secrets, and one was a place called Mystery Lake near a small gold camp called Rand on the far side of the mesa), the advantages of a good guide and the dangers of getting lost or being robbed, tales of bandits, an occasional mention of the rumored outlaw town of Rathole, and of course the odds against finding another gold strike like Bonanza.

It took Rocklin a while to find a mule that wasn't about to fall over dead, but he finally did. When he started south on a faint trail through endless stretches of green—pine, fir, spruce—he had axes, shovels, picks, extra handles, knives, guns, ammunition, canteens, extra clothing for warmth, soap, flour, and salt pork, beans and coffee, sugar and canned fruit, blankets and cooking utensils, a saw, hammer and nails, a washtub, a dismantled wheelbarrow, even a box of dynamite. Also some items he hoped would come in handy—a couple of bags of gold dust and some nuggets.

Rocklin didn't much like the deep forest. He had been a man of the sea and, later, the open West, ranch country. The forest gave him a closed-in feeling, even a blind feeling. The sun never showed through, and he couldn't see much beyond the trees closely surrounding him.

His thoughts kept drifting back to Manhattan and his quick trip home while Bannister was getting the reports together. He couldn't shake off the impressions, dogging him since Russell Junction, of the stark contrasts and, especially, the bizarre similarities between his home in the East and his endlessly vast home in the West. The sea, too, was his home. For a man with so many homes, he felt strangely detached at times.

He checked his compass. Often in the deep wilderness, when thoughts were wandering off course, the traveler was wandering off course, too. It could happen in an instant, just as in the city. Manhattan, now—it reminded him of Russell Junction. Alive and chaotic, with most of the population always coming and going, eager and brutal in the search for . . . whatever it was.

His wife had said, in her usual straight way, that if he was going to take the impossible job, it would be better if he wanted to take it.

"There's no one else," he had said. "I'm . . ." It sounded overweening even before it came out. He was *not* the only man who could handle it. That was absurd.

"You're their last resort," his wife had said. That was probably accurate.

"Keep planning our world trip," he had told her. "We'll leave in the fall. There's no point in starting out by crossing the Atlantic in the winter."

"I'll be ready when you are." Had she sounded . . . impersonal?

"Are the children asleep? I'll just look in on them."

He had left early so he could walk the two miles or so from the Village to Grand Central Depot.

From Washington Square he had walked straight up Fifth Avenue. There was movement and signs of movement everywhere, and he wondered how much longer there would be a Greenwich Village. Piers kept sticking out into the Hudson River farther and farther north, and the resulting light industry and warehouses kept pushing steadily at the Village's western boundary. Movement. Movement was the dominating force everywhere. Take Delmonico's. How many times had it joined the push uptown? He had passed where it used to be at 14th Street and Fifth Avenue, then he had passed it where it was now, at 26th Street and Fifth Avenue (he and his wife seldom ate there these days) and where will it go next? Where will it all go?

And Grand Central Depot, it was just like Russell Junction—steam trains dominated. North of the depot, Fourth Avenue was just a big ditch for trains, trains huffing smoke everywhere. Everything coming and going. Where was the West going? Why was he heading downhill? He was off course again.

He had been climbing gradually for three days, although one of the days was mostly wasted because of a heavy rain. He had waited it out under a quickly fashioned shelter in the heaviest cluster of big trees he could find. He had, in fact, stayed completely dry and even built a small fire for some hot coffee. He was sure he would break out of the trees soon and see the huge face of Rocky Mesa. It was a wet day with occasional sprinkles, and once or twice he thought he caught the sharp green smell of juniper. He could imagine it growing

16

among the rocks where the timberline gradually gave way to the higher altitude. It should be soon. He was feeling edgy, and so was Buck. The mule didn't care.

Rocklin decided to turn straight uphill. He hadn't gone more than a mile before the sky began to cast its light between the smaller and more scattered stands of evergreen. He found himself hurrying, or trying to, and stopped for a moment to look around. Buck spoke to him in a soft snort. He could glimpse the side of the mesa and, over the sounds of the forest, hear running water. He dismounted, trailed Buck's reins, and started toward the open area on foot, pausing every few steps to look and listen. The sound of the water was getting louder, and it was not flowing over rocks but splashing on them.

There was a small waterfall just ahead and to his left. He edged that way and saw the rocky open country and the fall. He stayed in among the trees and took his glasses out of the case. The fall was closer than it looked and the glasses brought it right in front of him. He caught a movement and turned his glasses to the south.

A rider was coming along the base of the cliff, heading right for the waterfall. He seemed close enough to touch. As Rocklin watched, the rider gave an odd lurch forward, and a second later there was the far-off boom of a heavy rifle. The man slipped from his saddle and hit the ground, his head bouncing just once.

Swiftly, Rocklin swung his binoculars farther south. He saw the sniper right away, on a high ledge of ground below the mesa. He was slipping his rifle into a saddle scabbard. Rocklin thought he must be at least three hundred and fifty yards away, but he would be coming down to make sure his victim was dead. Rocklin decided to take a chance. He slipped his glasses into the case, hung it on a limb, and moved quietly toward the open country. The killer was out of sight, apparently following a back trail off the ledge that took him behind a curve of the cliff.

Rocklin went into a crouch and ran toward a clump of juniper. He stopped to look for the sniper, didn't see him, and crept swiftly closer to the fallen man. Three more times he crouched and ran; two times he stopped for cover, and the third time he was at the man's side. The sniper was not yet in sight.

Rocklin turned the fallen man over, intending to search him, and was surprised to find him still breathing. He was dying, though. Rocklin lifted his head and he opened his eyes.

"You killed me," he said. "What happened?"

"Who are you?" Rocklin asked.

"I gave the signal."

"What signal?"

"One shot, like Big Nose Homer said. You waved me on. What happened?"

"I'm not the man who shot you. Why were you heading this way? Where's the trail?"

"You shouldn't have killed me," the man said, sounding as though his feelings had been hurt. Then he died.

Rocklin glimpsed the sniper coming along the

base of the cliff. He slipped the dead man's six-shooter out of its holster and took cover behind some rocks.

The sniper wasn't long in coming. He dismounted, walked the last few yards, and looked down at the body, touching it roughly with the toe of his boot. He hunkered down and went through his victim's pockets, finding some money and putting it into his own pocket. He saw that the dead man's gun was missing and looked around for it, puzzled. He stiffened, very slightly, but Rocklin caught the involuntary movement and knew that he had left some sign that gave him away.

The sniper stood up easily. There was blood on his hands and he wiped them on his denims and rested his right hand on the gun in his holster. He was still looking around casually for the missing gun when Rocklin stepped out from behind the rock and said, "Here it is."

The sniper's Colt cleared the holster in one swift movement. The man moved so fast and so decisively that Rocklin just had time to shoot him in the chest. And he had wanted to question him.

Rocklin tossed the gun on the ground beside its owner. He carefully obliterated all sign of his presence around the two bodies and along his track from the trees, hoping that it would rain again and finish the job so no one could doubt that the sniper had been killed by the man he had shot down.

Four

They came looking for the sentry the next day and followed his tracks to the bodies. They looked around, riding here and there, puzzled. Then they dismounted and saw what Rocklin had hoped they would see. They rounded up the dead men's horses, loaded the bodies, and tied them to the saddles. They stopped again at the waterfall, feeling uneasy. Then they left the two horses where they were and rode slowly north along the base of the cliff. As the sound of the fall grew fainter behind them, they could hear what sounded like chopping.

Rocklin saw them coming. He had expected them. He stopped chopping, picked up his rifle, and positioned himself behind a rock.

When the men were fifty yards away, they stopped to stare at a crude sign that had been pounded into the ground. It said "Trespassers Will Be Shot."

At that moment, Rocklin pulled the trigger, bouncing a chunk of lead off the side of the cliff. It made an intimidating sound as it screamed past the heads of the two hardcases. In the silence that followed, one of the men yelled, "Who the hell are you?"

"None of your business! Can't you read? Keep your hands away from those guns, or I'll put the next shot right between your eyes."

The men nudged their horses, starting to edge farther apart. With two quick shots Rocklin took both of their hats off.

"Don't try that again. I'll kill the next man who moves so much as an inch," he yelled. "Who are you? What do you want?"

"We're from Rathole. You can't stay here. This is Heller's territory." One of the men lurched suddenly sideways in his saddle, reaching for his rifle as he went down. Rocklin shot him dead.

"Heller? Who's Heller. And what's Rathole, the new state capital? I've got papers for this claim. What have you got?"

The outlaw stared down at his partner for a second, then shouted, "How long have you been here? Didn't you hear some shooting yesterday?"

"I heard it. None of my business. And what I do is none of your business. You can tell anyone else who might want to ride this way that he'll be met with a buffalo gun. Now get!"

The outlaw stared at Rocklin a long minute. What he saw was a scruffy miner with a sandy, gray-streaked beard staring back at him over the sights of a heavy rifle. "Get out or get killed," he yelled, and started to turn his horse.

"Take your partner," Rocklin shouted. "But stay where I can see you." He kept a bead on the man until he disappeared behind the rock and juniper along the rugged trail, then he made a dash for the taller trees of the deep forest, taking his glasses with him.

It wasn't hard to follow the rider leading the horse with his partner's body. He wondered about the man Heller and what his reaction would be when he saw his men dead. He might be hotheaded enough to send twenty or thirty of his men to rush the mine and kill Rocklin and have done with it; he might send a two- or three-man probe to find out just what was going on; or he might wait and take time to think it over, although that was unlikely. Whatever he did, it would give Rocklin a look into his mind—and some idea of the odds in favor of Rocklin's risky plan.

It was slow going. The horse with the body was skittish, and the outlaw had trouble leading it. He was not far away, and Rocklin, in among the trees, had no trouble keeping him in sight, but it was more than half an hour before he approached the waterfall.

Rocklin settled down against a tree, took out his glasses and watched the rider add the other two horses to the train. As the outlaw approached the waterfall, he stopped, looked carefully around, gazed up at the sentry rock above the Granite Pass trail, remembered that the sentry was not there, but lying dead across his saddle, and led the horses with the bodies straight into the waterfall.

Rocklin sat and thought about that for awhile. Then he thought some more as he made his way slowly back to the mine.

Dain Heller scowled at his second in command, whose name was Hank Bowdry. "There's nothing in that mine," he said. "Everybody knows that. He's been planted there. If he stays, he's bound to find the waterfall trail, sooner or later."

"What if he does? A lizard couldn't get up here alive, if we didn't want it to."

"Why didn't anyone see him? How did he walk in there without being spotted? Get Gantry, I want to walk to him."

"Gantry's dead."

"Yeah, that's right. But why? And who's this other man?"

"Looks like he could've been Red Breen. Big Nose sent word that he was coming. Lefty was on watch at the top of the waterfall trail. He said he couldn't see what went on down there, but it sounded to him like Red forgot to give the rest of the signal when he started for the fall, so Gantry shot him. Or maybe Big Nose forgot to give Red the rest of the signal. Who knows?"

"And Gantry?" Heller asked.

"It looks like he went down to see if Red was dead after he shot him and found out he

24

wasn't—quite."

"So some half-witted sourdough prospector shows up and nobody knows how he got here, and he ain't been here a full two days and already three men are dead. Go get him. I want to talk to him."

Five

They almost caught Rocklin off guard. He had been hard at work and hadn't expected them so soon. He was reminded again that bungling, along with false assumptions, could be very dangerous. Without knowing it, he had formed a mental picture of a high mesa that stretched for miles, where a person could get lost trying to find a small thieves' settlement called Rathole. That picture was shattered when he pushed his wheelbarrow filled with rock out into the open from the mine entrance and caught a movement fifty yards along the mesa wall toward the waterfall.

Four things happened at once: Rocklin dived for cover behind a rock; a man with a rifle pointed at him shouted, "Don't move"; another man, closing in, made a dash for better cover, and a third man, farther away, bounced a bullet off the rock that Rocklin had ducked behind.

The slug had hardly snarled away toward the trees before Rocklin was on the jump toward the cover he had chosen the day before, where his rifle was. It was only a few feet away, and his move was so swift that he was in position and firing before the three men could scramble to save their own skins. He paused to feed more cartridges into his Winchester and to remind himself that he might well be dead. Men had crawled out of Rathole in less than two hours, so where had he gotten the idea that the town was at least half a day away, hidden somewhere on the vast mesa? Did he want this job or not? He decided he had better act as if he did, if he wanted to get out of it alive.

The closest man yelled, "Hold your fire! We just want to talk."

"Then why sneak up on me?" Rocklin shouted back.

"Because, dammit, you're too quick on the trigger. We wanted to get the drop on you. Can you blame us?"

"All right, talk. But if anyone sticks his nose out I'll shoot it off."

"The boss wants to see you."

"What boss?"

"Our boss. The boss at Rathole. You know who I mean."

"I do not. And I don't want to. If he wants to see me, here I am."

"He told us to fetch you."

"Too bad. Tell him to come ahead if he wants to see me, but he'd better stop at the property line and give me a yell or I'll shoot him. It's posted. Now get going." Silence. No hint of movement.

Rocklin threw a shot at the man who had been talking. "I said get going!"

"Come on, mister," the man shouted. "What's it going to cost you? Heller's not going to like it, if we come back without you."

Rocklin laughed. "Too bad. If you're that scared of him, why go back at all? Go anywhere you want, but get off my property. Now!"

"Hold your fire, then," the man said. "We're going. But you'll come to see him, if he has to send fifty men after you."

"Shut up, stupid!" one of the other men yelled. "Let's get out of here."

Rocklin went back to work clearing the rocks and other debris out of the mine. It helped stretch his muscles and clear his mind, and he welcomed it. He had scouted the mine thoroughly the day before and had found it a poor excuse for a mine but an excellent place to hole up. The main entrance into the side of the mesa wasn't very deep, not much more than twenty feet, but it was high enough to stand up in and almost twelve feet wide, a good site for the back end of his cabin. Farther north along the cliff he had found the remains of an unfinished structure that was obviously meant to support a crusher. The thing was falling apart, but there were some usable planks and beams. He would pound together a rough sled and use the mule for dragging the heavier material—plus enough timber for a secure place to live—to the mine entrance. With the front of the cabin overlooking the trail from the waterfall, and the back built into the mine, it would be hard for anyone to approach without risking his neck.

The good thing about it was that someone had tried to cut a lateral, or crosscut tunnel, from the back of the shallow mine to another entrance the other side of the crusher. This entrance, farther along the cliff, was not really a mine at all, but merely a large hole, or cave, in the sheer rock side of the mesa, and because of the rough irregularity of the cliff, the opening faced mostly north, away from the waterfall trail and out of the sight of the lookout on the ledge above Granite Pass Road.

With a fence made of four-inch-thick trees and limbs stretched in a half circle around the entrance, it would be a perfect place for Buck and the mule. There was even a small stream coming out of a cleft in the cliff a little farther on. And if Rocklin could get the crosscut tunnel cleaned out, he would have an emergency escape route from the back of his cabin to the makeshift stable. It might take three or four weeks of hard work to get it all done, but in the meantime he was well situated, and he knew he couldn't ask for a better position for getting on Heller's nerves.

The real problem was the crosscut tunnel. It was small and it was a mess. The men who had worked the mine had used dynamite so carelessly that the crosscut was unsafe; then they had tried to fix it with inadequate timbering. Rocklin thought it could be made usable, but it would be slow and dangerous work. And nowhere had he seen the slightest sign of gold.

"He can't be a prospector," Dain Heller said. He was angry, dangerously angry. His men recognized it as the stubborn, sullen kind of anger that boiled up inside their boss at the slightest hint of opposition, and they were fidgeting.

"He sure acts like one," said the man, called Rex, who had done most of the talking to Rocklin.

"Wouldn't he have to?" Heller demanded. "I tell you he's a Pinkerton, or some other kind of agent. He's just smarter than the others. Only he picked the wrong dodge."

"What do you mean?"

"I mean there ain't no gold in that hole, that's what I mean. Have you ever kicked through that pile of rocks down there? Have you picked up a handful of tailing and sifted it through your fingers? I tell you, there ain't a sign of gold, no quartz, nuthin!" He stared balefully at his men and they shifted on their feet. "You said he could shoot."

"Lots of men can shoot," Rex said, trying to stand up to his boss.

"Why didn't you bring him, then?" Rex had no answer.

"He was holed up," one of the other men said. "He could have picked us off one by one."

"So he *can* shoot," Heller insisted.

The third man, the one who had told Rex to shut up down at the mine, said, "He doesn't hit anything except what he aims at. It'll take more than three men to bring him back. Rex here told him we could come at him with fifty."

Heller swung at Rex, knocking him sprawling into a corner of the room. Rex went for his gun and Heller kicked it out of his hand, then took out a knife and went for the man's throat.

But there was a fifth man in the room, Hank Bowdry, who was always at Heller's side when the boss was dealing with his men. Bowdry grabbed Heller's arm and said, "Wait, Dain. We've lost three men already. If that miner's an enemy, let's not do his killing for him. Rex might be dumb, but he's on our side."

Heller didn't say anything to Bowdry, or even look at him, but he pulled back and sheathed his knife. "If I ever hear of you opening your mouth again, I'll finish what I started," he told Rex. "Now get out of here, all three of you." He brooded awhile after his men shuffled out, then told Bowdry. "We can't let him stay there."

"Specially if he's a spy," Bowdry agreed.

"The longer he's there . . . Pick fifteen or twenty men. Go down tomorrow morning before light and get him out of there. Shoot the place to pieces if you have to. Kill him . . . There ain't any chance he'd have a posse down there?"

"No. We'd have got word. You know, Dain, if he is looking for gold, and if he really doesn't have any idea what he's wandered into, he might act just the way he is acting. Some of these sourdoughs are pretty crusty old jaspers. He could kick up a helluva fuss. You might give some thought to just leaving him be."

"No. I don't like the smell of it. If he's what I think he is, he might act the same way, mightn't he? And that means he's too damn smart for his own good. If you can bring him back, all right. If not, kill him. I'll kill him anyway, after he talks."

Six

Rocklin worked swiftly. By nightfall he had a crude one-rail fence around the large open cave, and had pulled enough high grass to last Buck and the mule a night or two. He had also erected two four-by-six uprights at the entrance to the mine where his cabin would be. With the help of the mule, he had pulled a twelve-foot, four-by-eight beam into place that he could secure on top of the uprights as the basic structure of the shelter. He also pounded together two crude sawhorses, about three feet high, that would help him lift the beam into place one end at a time, first to the sawhorses, and then to the uprights the following day.

He built a fire in the dark, opened a can of pork and beans, and made some coffee. He had been thinking about the men at Rathole all day, off and on, and as he finished his coffee he made up his mind.

He gathered all the tools he had been using and stashed them in the crosscut behind a pile of rocks, piling more rocks into the entrance so no one would bother to look in, rolled his personal gear into his bedroll, and doused the fire. Then he went to the stable, saddled Buck, put a halter on the mule, and led them into the woods, covering his tracks as best he could in the dark.

It began to drizzle, and Rocklin welcomed it. Buck would roam free and stay clear of any human creature, except Rocklin. He staked the mule a mile deep in the piney woods. He made his way north along the face of the mesa and found a vantage point several feet up on a shelf of rock.

From his years at sea, Rocklin knew the trick of not trying to see anything straight on in the deep darkness. Instead, he would let his eyes wander without any particular aim, and objects would appear slightly to the side of his focus, picked up by his peripheral vision in the night. He settled down to watch. He wasn't sure they would come; he only knew they might, tonight or some night soon. He dozed.

He heard them before he saw them. The clouds that had drifted down through Granite Pass and settled over the forest during the night were moving east toward the flatland, taking the drizzle with them, and the deep blackness was turning a dirty gray. Buck, who had grazed closer to Rocklin's vantage point early in the night and then stood sleeping, snorted, alerting Rocklin, and moved farther into the evergreen.

The outlaws were trying to be quiet, but it was not easy in the dim light. Rocklin could clearly hear rustles and stumbles, and by the time it was light enough to see, he knew pretty much where to look. They were strung out, as many as twenty of them, just inside the timberline, surrounding the campsite. They meant to take him this time—or kill him.

It was a matter of patience, and the outlaws didn't have very much. When it had been light less than an hour, and no sound or movement had been detected at Rocklin's camp, one of the men yelled for him to come out. There was no hint of reply.

"We know you're there, sourdough! You're going to see the boss, or you're going to die in that hole! It's up to you!" The silence deepened. When it had stretched beyond the gang's ability to listen, there was movement. They were deciding what to do and sending a man back and forth along the line to pass the word.

Rocklin thought they might send a couple of men his way to scout his camp from the north side, or at least see how close they could get. They already knew how dangerous it was to approach from the direction of the waterfall. But Rocklin had been lucky in choosing the mine as his approach to Heller. The face of the mesa north of the site appeared unbroken to an observer in the woods, and the other mine entrance was hidden from sight. Rocklin stayed where he was, hoping they wouldn't come. He wanted the cave and the stable for Buck and the mule to remain a secret as long as possible. He was confident that he could outflank any scouts that were sent and kill them quietly with his knife. In fact, the way the men were strung out among the trees made them all easy targets for a quiet man with a knife who had explored that neck of the woods and knew it well. But he didn't want to start that kind of war of attrition. There was, he hoped, a better way.

There was more yelling now. They had decided not to risk a reconnaisance. They were moving closer to the camp, using what cover they could find. They had decided to force him out, the safe way.

"All right!" one of the men yelled, "this is your last chance to come out of there, or we drive you out!" He threw a shot into the cavelike entrance to the mine. It was not a bad plan, as long as they had enough men and guns—simply blast away at the opening and the lead would ricochet off the hard-rock sides and top of the cave and fly every which way.

The booming and cracking thunder of the guns seemed to last an hour, although it was more like five minutes. Rocklin thought that even if there wasn't any gold in the hole, someone could come along and make a lead mine out of it.

The firing eased off and stopped. The dead silence rang with echoes, then the echoes eased off, leaving only the silence. The gunmen stayed put. Then a voice yelled, "Give him some more!" and the shattering noise lasted another few minutes. It was enough. Hank Bowdry called three names and said, "Go up and see what's left of him." The three men moved in carefully, taking no chances. They had seen dead men shoot before. Rocklin lost sight of them behind the curving side of the mesa as they neared his camp.

The silence didn't last as long this time. A demanding and impatient voice shouted, "What's going on?"

"Hold your horses," was the shouted reply. More time passed, then a man showed himself at the mine entrance. "He's not here!"

"What do you mean, he's not there!"

"I mean he's not here! Looks like he's pulled out."

Rocklin listened to the angry cussing with a certain satisfaction. It was going to work.

The gunmen didn't have to search the mine entrance all that thoroughly; there was nothing and no one there; and that was that. They didn't even bother to look behind the rock pile that obscured the entrance to the crosscut tunnel.

Hank Bowdry cussed some more and told his men to go on back to Rathole and tell Heller what they had found. "Slim and I will be along pretty soon," he said. "I want to look around. Maybe we can pick up a trail. Make sure he's gone."

"It's pretty wet," one of his men observed.

"We'll try anyway. Dain will want to know. He had a hunch that this man was no fool. Get going."

Rocklin watched Bowdry and Slim as they went over the area around his camp, and he was glad that it had drizzled. Otherwise they would surely have found some sign. But they didn't range far north of his hiding place, and he was glad of that. The makeshift stable and corral were still safe. But Bowdry did decide to knock down the uprights that Rocklin had worked to put in place.

It didn't matter. Rocklin had had the better part of a day and a night to think about his original plan and had decided to change it. He wouldn't go to the trouble of building a combination cabin and fort, because he had decided the job wouldn't take as long as he had thought it would. He would disappear for a day or two, take Buck and the mule into Russell Junction and come back with enough heavy tarpaulin for a tent, some more grub, and feed for the animals. He would place the tent where the cabin would have been and use the planks to support a simple log wall at the front of the shelter as a bulwark. Then he would "work" the mine and concentrate on the one thing he now wanted most—to get a look at the top of the mesa.

When Bowdry and Slim reported to Heller that they had found nothing, the boss still wasn't satisfied. "Keep an eye on the place," he ordered in his slow-talking way. He thought a minute and added, "Tell Big Nose to keep an eye out. I want to know if the miner shows up in Pine Hollow." After further thought he added, "If he doesn't, I want to know that, too."

Rocklin stayed overnight in Russell Junction, taking a day to get cleaned up, have some laundry done, and visit the office of the sectional superintendent of the railroad, where he took his time studying maps of the area. He also decided he might need a couple of coal oil lanterns and a miner's carbide lamp.

There was time for talk, too, at the combination barbershop and bathhouse. He felt like a different man when he started for his camp the next day.

He decided to follow the Russell Junction-Pine Hollow stage road for awhile before cutting up through the forest, partly because it was easier, and partly because he wanted to find out if a certain stranger he had seen in town was as curious about Rocklin as he seemed.

He had first noticed the man when he was having dinner in a restaurant the day before. The man was trying to watch him without appearing to, and he wasn't very good at it. Rocklin was mildly curious, but not concerned. The man was no Western outlaw; he seemed to be young and a little green for this country.

Rocklin had dismissed the young man from his mind until he had found him on his trail as he left town. Now he was more curious.

He kept to the road for several miles before taking to the woods, and when he did, he made sure he was not in sight of the man behind him. He waited in the dark shadows of the trees. There was no doubt about it; the man spotted his trail into the trees, and even stopped for a moment to make sure, but he didn't follow. He was on his way to Pine Hollow and that was that.

Was it simple curiosity? Rocklin didn't think so, but he did not have a feeling of danger—none, that is, except the danger of being known by anyone.

When he was in sight of his mine, he made a light camp in the forest, brewed some coffee, and waited until the dark hours of the morning to walk the animals to the corral and settle down in his bedroll at the back of his cave. At mid-morning he was busy putting up his big tent, and by noon he was busy chopping wood.

Seven

When Heller's men reported that the miner was back he just nodded, as though he wasn't surprised. The men waited for instructions, which were, as usual, slow in coming. "Watch him. Keep watching him. What's he doing?"

"Chopping wood. Looks like he plans to stay awhile."

Heller nodded again. "The lookout didn't see him." It was a statement.

"Nope."

"Ain't never seen him, coming or going."

"Nope."

"He's too careful. Watch him."

It gave Rocklin time to finish his camp and clean out the crosscut tunnel between the camp and the corral. It was hard and dangerous work, and he proceeded with care. When he had a passage he could crawl through, he inspected it foot by foot, and decided it could be enlarged with a little work and a minimum of risk. And it would be an escape route.

There was a puzzling thing about it, though. Just where the crosscut intersected with Buck's cave, there was an overhead hole in the rock. He had chipped away at it when he was cleaning the tunnel to make sure it was solid, and a quarter ton of debris had come tumbling down at him.

He wondered if the men who had been there before thought they had found a vein. But there was no vein. There wasn't a fault; there wasn't a seam. There didn't seem to be anything but solid rock. Could they have been drilling an airhole? Not likely. Not this close to the entrance cave; there was no need for it at all.

He widened the hole and chiseled some climbing holes into the side of it so he could inspect it more closely, on the chance that the man or men who cut it had some rational purpose in mind. As he chipped away at the top of the hole, the rock seemed to be softer, more porous. Then he felt the wetness. He climbed down at once to think it over.

There was water deep in the rocks of the mesa; that much was certain. There were a number of places where water had run down the cliffs from cracks or seams along its side, probably when snow was melting. There was the small stream not far along the cliff from the corral, and there was the big stream at the waterfall. And water was always something to be aware of when a structure like the mesa was being drilled or blasted into. Unexpected water had drowned many a man working in a mine. There could even be a reservoir, a small lake in fact, under the mesa.

The man who cut that hole might have been trying to find a way to the top of the mesa when he ran into signs of water and stopped. If Rocklin had thought of finding another way to the top, someone else might have. It was the only reasonable explanation he could think of for that hole. But suppose the water was not trapped in the rock, but was from an existing streambed? A streambed up on the mesa that the mysterious hole-digger had known about? Rocklin had pounded together a crude bunk in a back corner of his tent and stretched canvas across it. He rolled in that night thinking about that inexplicable vertical hole in the useless mine.

A couple of Heller's men showed up the next day. They rode all around the boundaries of the camp with the clear intent of annoying Rocklin, but he didn't care if they rode around in a circle all day, although he did throw a couple of shots at them when they ventured too close—just to let them know he still didn't want trespassers wandering onto his claim. When he went into the trees to cut wood for the front wall of his tent shelter, the men made a point of watching him, but didn't crowd him.

There were different men the next day, and different ones the day after that, all of them going through the same routine—watching all the time and occasionally coming too close—whereupon Rocklin would put a shot or two close enough to their skulls to make them duck and keep their distance.

Work at the phony mine progressed. The front wall of his tent was in place and solidly braced, and it was far enough out from the mine entrance so Rocklin could see the surrounding area clearly through three gunholes. The mine was cleared of rock, and the corral was within quick reach through the crosscut level of the mine.

The watching gunmen had still not discovered the corral; they had never seen Rocklin venture that far along the mesa wall, so they hadn't bothered to look. Rocklin knew he could never drop his guard and be sure of staying alive, so he was always up before dawn so he could see when the outlaws approached from the direction of the waterfall trail. He would watch them from the woods, where they couldn't spot him, then slip out from among the trees and return to his camp by way of the corral. He would emerge from his tent at the same time each morning, so the spies thought they knew just when he rolled out, cooked breakfast, and started to work. He knew from experience that an established habit could be an advantage, because a sudden break from it could catch an enemy by surprise.

One morning when he was watching the darkness lift, he saw a rider appear briefly at the edge of the forest and then quickly draw back into the shadows. He hadn't been looking straight at the place where it happened, but he knew he hadn't imagined it.

His first thought was that they had decided to stop playing games with him and either take him to Heller or kill him. His second thought was that someone might be trying to approach his camp without being seen by the ever-present sentry on the ledge. If it was the outlaws, they had come earlier than usual; but they would if they wanted to catch him sleeping, and they would also close in from the woods because they could get closer to the camp that way without being seen.

But something—maybe the rider's quick movement to get back out of sight—made Rocklin think that some stranger was trying to sneak into his camp. He took nothing for granted, though. He took his glasses with him and changed his vantage point—taking care not to be seen from any direction—so he could keep both the trees and the waterfall trail in plain sight.

Whatever the man wanted, Rocklin would have to think about it twice. If he warned the man with a shot and then ordered him to get out or be killed, the outlaws would know they were being watched more closely than they were watching Rocklin. It was an advantage that Rocklin didn't want to lose. But if he let the rider—any rider—get too close without challenging him, and the outlaws got wind of it, they would wonder why.

Rocklin decided he would have to let the intruder get all the way into his camp, and shoot him, as though he had been surprised while asleep—or talk to him first and then shoot him.

The daylight was coming fast, and the next time the strange rider came out from among the trees for a quick look around, Rocklin glimpsed him clearly through his glasses. The man had dismounted and left his horse out of sight, and he was dressed differently, but Rocklin recognized him as the rider who had followed him out of Russell

47

Junction. He was no outlaw.

Rocklin watched him approach the camp. The man stayed under cover until he was close enough to speak in a normal voice and be heard by anyone in the tent. But he had passed Rocklin's hiding place on his way to the camp, and Rocklin was now behind him.

When the intruder, confident that he had not been seen, stepped into the open and said, "Hello. In the camp. I want to talk to you," Rocklin swore under his breath, crept swiftly up behind the man, and hustled him roughly through the double-flap entrance of the tent. He pushed him onto the bunk, took out the double-action .38 from his shoulder holster and pressed the muzzle against the man's forehead.

"I'm going to have to kill you, son," Rocklin said.

The young man was not intimidated. "My name's Riddle. I'm here to help," he said. "I work for the railroad."

"This is my claim and I don't need any help," Rocklin growled. "What railroad? I don't have any partners in this. Make sense, and quick!"

"Flanagan told me they were sending someone, and I heard some talk in Pine Hollow about a crazy miner. I just put two and two together."

Rocklin had heard Flanagan's name. He was the top troubleshooter for the railroad and was a little-known, shadowy figure, the railroad's equivalent of Bannister. It was possible that someone working for Heller knew the name Flanagan, but very unlikely. He found himself getting very angry, but

48

he reminded himself that he had known all along that there would probably be a leak from someone at the "highest level" meeting. Nevertheless . . . "Time's up," he said, "Get out or get shot."

Riddle headed out, protesting all the way. "But there are things you ought to know."

"Stay out of sight," Rocklin said. "Go out the way you came in." He took out his knife. "And don't talk above a whisper." It was getting lighter, and Heller's men would be showing up any time. Rocklin was carrying his rifle in one hand, the knife in the other, and his Colt under his arm.

"Big Nose is working for Heller," Riddle said.

"Just keep walking. Angle down toward the trees now. Don't you know there's a lookout on that ledge at the pass? If it had been a little lighter, you might be dead right now. Stay out of his line of sight, and don't even look his way. If you do just what I tell you, you might get out of this alive."

"I know about the lookout. I cut across through the trees. Listen—"

"Shut up." Rocklin was listening. He had heard a faint noise, something that sounded like a rock being dislodged by a careless step. He waited, but there was nothing else. There was something he wanted to know, but he certainly didn't want to question the hapless railroad dick. "Don't talk anymore." he ordered.

"But Big Nose is the deputy sheriff in Pine Hollow." It was the answer to the question in Rocklin's mind: Why shouldn't Big Nose work for Heller? And there was not one mention of Big Nose in all the reports Rocklin had read.

49

"I wanted to tell Big Jim Haggard, but I haven't seen him around town since he got back from Chicago."

So Riddle had been around town for some time, which almost certainly meant that Heller knew he was a special agent of some kind. Again, Rocklin had to bring his anger under control.

"Son," he said, "I don't have any idea what you're talking about." He didn't add that he would have to do something about it if he had the least indication that anyone had seen him talking to Riddle. He didn't actually want to kill the young man, although he doubted that he would stay alive very long anyway. He decided he couldn't take the chance that he was not seen talking to him. He would let him head for the trees, yell for him to get out and stay out, and shoot to wound. He had a feeling it wouldn't fool Heller, but if there was a witness, and the witness was fooled, that would be something—not much, but something.

They reached the last rocky cover, and the timberline was a short distance away. It was light now, although the sun wasn't showing.

"Get going," Rocklin said.

Riddle hesitated. "Well," he said, "whoever you are, just remember I'm in town, if I can be of any help."

"It doesn't matter who I am, does it?" Rocklin said. "I could be a dead man now, anyway." The young man stared at Rocklin a moment, and when the meaning of the remark hit him, he looked almost stricken. He started to look around to see if anyone could be watching, but thought better of it. He didn't look at Rocklin again, but broke into a run and headed for the trees.

The situation was simple. Rocklin knew he had to assume that Heller knew about the young agent in town, since Riddle had made it clear that he had revealed his identity to Big Nose and had then found out that the deputy sheriff was working for Heller. He also had to assume that if Heller found out that Riddle had slipped off in the night, he would suspect that the agent had made contact with someone. And Heller would take Riddle and make him talk—one way or another.

As Rocklin was lifting his rifle, he caught another sound, and this time there was a slight movement to go with it. He whirled to his right, looking toward the waterfall, and there, less than fifty yards away, were two of Heller's men. They were on foot. There was no doubt that they had left their horses behind and had crept forward to see what was going on. As soon as Rocklin spotted them they headed for the fall, dodging for cover all the way.

Rocklin started to shoot, but they were moving fast and he knew that any shot would attract the attention of the lookout on the ledge. But he also knew he had to cut them off, stop them from reporting to Heller.

He made a dash for the fall, and for cover that would protect him from the sniper on the ledge. But he didn't have a chance to pick his cover; Heller's men were getting too close to the fall. His shots stopped them dead in their tracks, winging them both, but a second later he heard and felt a chunk of lead growl past his ear, and a split second later came the boom of a buffalo gun. He moved quickly and found cover just ahead of another chunk of lead.

The two men heading for the fall could almost have made it, if they had moved when Rocklin did, but they were bleeding, and not eager to get out in the open for even a little while.

Rocklin knew where they were, and that they would have to try to reach the fall and their horses sooner or later. He wanted to get between them and the fall, or as close to between as possible, and at the same time stay out of the sniper's line of fire. He took plenty of time, making no unnecessary or sudden moves.

A half hour passed, an hour. Finally, Rocklin was where he wanted to be, and the outlaws had to be wondering if that last shot from the ledge had found its mark. The sniper must be wondering too.

The silence stretched. Then Rocklin heard two things almost at the same time—the sound of a horse approaching from Granite Pass Road, and a clear voice from a few yards away saying, "This bleeding ain't stopping. We got to get out of here. He's dead."

"He's not dead," another voice stated positively.

"Whether he is or not, we can't stay here forever, can we?"

"We won't have to. Gage is on his way."

"How do you know?"

"Because he would be, dammit! Keep quiet!"

The sniper had dismounted and was making his way as quietly as he could toward the waterfall, but Rocklin could hear every step on the rocky trail. He waited until he knew exactly where the man was, stood up suddenly, and shot him between the eyes with his Winchester. He had not quite made cover again when a shot from a handgun behind him grazed his shoulder and tore the rifle from his hands. He spun around, going for the .38 under his arm. The two outlaws were trying to do two things at once—kill him and make it to the waterfall—and it was more than they could handle. While they were getting off a couple of shots apiece, Rocklin was taking care to shoot them both dead.

Then he stopped and thought awhile. He needed Buck. No, Buck was too fine a horse for a crazy miner. He needed the mule. He had to see the town on that mesa, and today was the day.

Eight

The waterfall was steep and crooked. A hundred, or two hundred, years ago it had been the rocky bed of a wider stream fed by springs deeply imbedded in the cracks of the huge mesa and replenished year-round by melting ice and snow. Now the streams that converged to make the falls had cut deeper into the rock, and the trail was a shelf two or three feet above the rushing water.

Twice, Rocklin had to make the horses carrying the bodies jump the stream from a narrowing shelf on one side to a wider shelf on the other. It wasn't easy going, but the mule was a climber. It took almost an hour, though, and Rocklin realized that the town of Rathole must be even closer to the edge of the mesa than he had figured.

The lookout at the top of the trail was so dumbfounded to see a mounted stranger leading three horses with bodies tied across their saddles that he had to recover before he pulled a rifle from his saddle scabbard, cocked it, and pointed it at

Rocklin's head.

"Who are you?" he croaked. "And you'd better have the right answer."

"I'm the miner who keeps having to kill trespassers, who do you think? I'm taking these dead men into town to have a talk with your boss, who already said he wants to see me. I can't work a gold mine if I'm constantly fighting off his men. You can come with me or you can stay here, but I'm going." Rocklin pulled his coat aside with both hands. "I'm not carrying a gun."

The lookout didn't dismount to examine the bodies, apparently recognizing them. He lowered the hammer of his rifle but didn't put it away. He followed as Rocklin headed up the trail.

The town wasn't much more than a mile away, although it was more of a scattered settlement than a town. There was a central building, a rickety, rambling affair that looked as though it had started as a storage shed and grown room by room over months or years until it covered a couple of thousand square feet. It even had additions on top of additions, at one place reaching a ramshackled three stories. Other shacks of various sizes were scattered more or less at random over the landscape for a quarter of a mile around. They all faced in different directions, so it was hard to tell if there was any kind of street that connected parts of the town. Several shacks were actually built with their backs to the town, revealing nothing to their neighbors but a narrow back door, a stoop, and a zinc or copper washtub hanging by a nail on the back wall. The outhouses were closer to the dwellings than they should have been and Rocklin decided that the outlaws didn't much care for the endless winter job of keeping a path open through the snow. There were some porches on houses facing the central structure, but not with chairs. It was strange; people came together to form a town of sorts, but wanted no neighbors. There was no color at all. Everything, the houses, the ground, the rocks and the scattered juniper, was weather-beaten gray.

Men gathered to watch silently as Rocklin's procession approached the big building. A few women peered briefly from doorways, and Rocklin saw a couple of children being jerked unceremoniously inside. The people seemed gray, too.

Near the main structure there were old racks for stretching hides, only now there were no hides, just two men. One of them was obviously dead. He was slack and twisted in the leather thongs tied around his wrists and ankles, and his mouth was open and ants were crawling in and out. The other man squirmed occasionally in his bonds, trying to relieve his dull agony.

Four men walked out of the main house and confronted Rocklin as he drew up. They stared at him silently.

Rocklin stared back for a minute, then, without being asked, got off the mule and stepped toward the men. "What does a man have to do to be left alone around here," he said. "Do you think I have nothing to do but fight off trespassers?" No answer. "Who is this Heller? I've been told he wants to see me. Well? What's the matter? Haven't you ever heard of him?"

One of the men took a step toward him. "I'm Dain Heller," he said. "Just who are you? Besides being the world's biggest fool, and a dead one at that."

Rocklin was not surprised. From sketchy descriptions, and especially from the man's manner, he had known who he was. He examined him casually for a moment and, although he knew it didn't show on his face, he was jolted.

He had seen the type before, once or twice, and it was the most dangerous kind of man he knew, the kind of man who totally lacked any sense of humanity, his own or anyone else's.

Early in his life, when Rocklin was an ordinary seaman on one of his father's ships, he had watched such a man from a distance and had decided the only thing to do was stay as far away from him as possible. Then one night, when the weather was rough and getting rougher, he bumped against the man while they were climbing down after taking in sail, just bumped against him, and the man came at him with a knife. Rocklin kicked him in the knee, and felt it give. At that moment, a wave buried the bow and took the man overboard. It would have taken Rocklin, too, if he hadn't seen it coming. He raised the cry of man overboard, but there was nothing anyone could do. Rocklin never told anyone what had happened, and if anyone had seen it, they had kept quiet. Now here he was again; same man, different name.

Heller was tall, at least six inches taller than

Rocklin, and he was nothing but lanky bone and muscle. Big hands, big feet, big joints and a big face, sharp Adam's apple, and hair growing every which way from a big head.

Rocklin smiled, a fairly nasty smile, considering the circumstances. "For accepting your invitation to visit? It seems to me you've been wanting my company pretty badly." Heller was silent. "I'm the man who owns that mine down there, free and clear and legally. The claim is recorded. And you're the fool, Heller. Here you are sitting on millions of dollars in gold, and you have the men to get it out and a man who knows how, and all you want to do is kill that man."

"You're a liar. There ain't no gold—"

Rocklin hit him. He didn't want to. He was risking sudden death and he knew it, but he was selling a certain image, a story, and he knew from experience that he had to go all the way, because, as dangerous as that was, it wasn't as dangerous as going only halfway.

Heller rocked back and went down on one knee, braced himself with one hand on the ground, and then got up very deliberately. There wasn't the slightest change in his expression.

Men moved back to give them room. Rocklin had the vivid impression that no one was very excited about this. They seemed more bored than anything.

Heller wasn't a fistfighter. He was a bear that just wanted to get hold of its prey and squeeze.

That was fine with Rocklin. He dodged Heller's first lunge and said, "If you had any brains you'd stop calling me a liar and listen." The second lunge was a little harder to escape, but Rocklin knew more than one trick. He retrieved his left arm by ducking quickly around Heller, twisting his bony hand in a painful way, and landing a solid chop to his right kidney. Heller paused for a second, but despite his surprise, his expression didn't change.

"All I need is some manpower, and we'll both be rich men," Rocklin said. Heller kept circling. "The man who worked that mine before didn't know what he was doing." Heller charged. Rocklin barely escaped, but he had the man's measure now. If he charged that way again, Rocklin could throw him twenty feet on his head. "Look. Let me show you something." Rocklin took out a small leather pouch of dust and nuggets. Heller kept coming. Rocklin turned to the man who had been closest to Heller when the four men met him. It was Hank Bowdry. "Can't anyone talk sense to this big nitwit?" He eluded Heller again, but it was close. The man was getting smarter, and he would grab Rocklin sooner or later. "Here, take a look at this." Rocklin tossed the pouch to Bowdry. Heller was tired of messing around. He took out a knife, an Arkansas toothpick about as heavy as a meat cleaver, and charged at Rocklin with his arms spread, as though he intended to wrap him up. Then he went flying over Rocklin's shoulder and landed against a rock, splitting his scalp a little. A trickle of blood was running down his jawline from under his bushy hair when he picked himself up, sheathed his knife, and walked toward Rocklin.

"How did you do that, sonny?" he asked. Rocklin was easily ten years older than the brute.

"Are you ready to listen?"

"Not about gold. There ain't any. Show me how you did that."

"Yes, there is. I've found gold in a dozen places, all over the world. Anyway, I didn't do it. You did."

"Are you trying to have fun with me?" He took out his knife again. "I'll hang you by the heels and gut you like a hawg."

"What for? It won't get you anything. Listening to me will. It was your own weight and momentum that made you fly through the air. I just put the pressure in the right place. Like a lever."

"Look at this, Dain," Bowdry said, offering the bag of gold.

Heller took the bag and dumped the contents into his big hand. "This didn't come from down there," he said.

"Yes, it did," Rocklin said.

"Then how come Haggard didn't find any?"

"Haggard, whoever he is, didn't know how."

"He found some at Rand."

"Rand? On the other side of the mesa? I've heard of it. It's a placer operation, isn't it? I'm talking about hardrock mining. It's a lot different. You have to know what you're looking at. The man who started those holes where I am, simply didn't know."

Dain Heller hunkered down and stared thoughtfully at the gold in his hand, stirring it with a

61

finger. His feet were flat on the ground and his rump was resting on his heels, almost touching the ground. His knees stuck up next to his chest and his upper arms rested on the knees. He reminded Rocklin of a squatting orangutan. Rocklin had seen only one other man who sat like that, a seaman on one of his ships, long ago. The seaman had come from the Arkansas hills.

Heller studied the gold a long time, then he looked up at Rocklin and smiled. "There could be one little hitch."

Rocklin didn't like the smile. He thought for the first time that he had lost his gamble.

"You could be the special agent sent by the big shots."

Rocklin studied Heller's expression while the seconds seemed to stretch into minutes. He started to say, "What special agent?" but he knew the smile would only get bigger if he did. There was only the slimmest of chances, hardly any chance at all, but he had no choice but to take it.

He laughed. "You're as mean and dangerous as an Arkansas razorback, Heller." The smile faded. "And believe me, if there were any way to do this without you, I'd drop you like a hot rock."

No one said anything. They just gazed at their victim.

"All right," Rocklin said. "I'm an agent. I mean I was an agent. The minute I knew what was in that hole down there, I quit working for those big shots, and getting nothing but the short end of the stick. I'm talking about gold, man. Gold!

"Sure, I know about you. I know *all* about you.

I've studied every report written about you in the past five years. And do you think I just rode up here, unarmed, to get my throat cut? Think, Heller! If you have any brain at all, think. I could have cleared out when twenty of your men came after me. Anyone but a crazy man would have, and you know it. *But I'm not giving up this gold!*

"You have thirty thousand dollars on your head. Your men have a total of about fifty thousand—"

"And you've killed six of them."

"I could have killed a dozen more, the way they were spread out along that timberline. And none of them would have known what hit them. But here I am. And for one reason. I *need* you."

"But I don't need you."

"Oh yes you do. Are you suddenly going to turn honest and go into the mining business right out in the open?" Heller was silent. "But the main reason you need me is that I know where the gold is and how to get it out."

There was a chance now. Heller wasn't sold, by any means, but he was listening.

"Did you ever take a look at the side of this mesa from a distance?" Heller was waiting. "It's as plain as the map of Texas if you know what you're looking at. This is not one big solid rock. You can look around you right here and see all kinds of cracks and crevices that have filled up with dust and dirt and seeds and other organic material so that juniper grows out of them. There's even some scrubby pine. What does all that tell you? That the strata are almost vertical." Heller was scowling at him now, and Rocklin wasn't sure what that meant.

"You've seen mesas south of here, out in the desert where the strata, I mean the layers, are flat, stacked on top of each other." Some of the men nodded, but Heller was still just listening. "But the solid rocks in this mesa—I mean big rocks, mountain-size—are jammed up against each other, so the layers are more up and down. I don't know how. Nobody does. Maybe by some great earthquake thousands of years ago.

"But one thing I do know—the men who started that mine down there didn't have the slightest idea what they were looking at, or how to get the gold out. They didn't know, or care, whether the structure was vertical or horizontal or crossways. They just blasted away, and they were damn lucky not to have buried themselves under a thousand tons of rock."

The living man tied to the rack groaned. Heller glanced his way, and then got up and went to him. He took out his knife and shoved it up under the man's ribs. When he came back, he said to Bowdry, "See they're taken down and buried." He glanced at Rocklin, saw the question on his face, and explained, "They stole firewood. Can't have that." He handed Rocklin the bag of gold and said, "Show me how you did that throw."

Firewood. Of course. There certainly wasn't much around. Not many sheds, actually. Some were separated from their houses but still close by, and others were attached, probably accessible from inside the shacks. Some of the outlaws undoubtedly left for warmer places during the worse parts of the winter, but the ones who stayed would die without firewood.

"Later," Rocklin said. "I've got work to do. That gold's not going to pile out of that rock like gravel."

"You said you could use my men," Heller said.

"When I'm ready. It'll be a couple of weeks at least. Then we'll draw up partnership papers."

"A handshake ought to do," Heller said, wanting to make an issue of it.

"But it won't. We need something in writing, giving every man who works the mine a share. Haven't you heard of the strikes up north? We don't want to invite trouble. Nobody will work for wages; we'll all be part-owners. You of all people ought to understand the difference between risk-taking and wage-earning. Right?" Heller didn't think it was funny. "I'll let you know when I'm ready," Rocklin said. He mounted the mule and started to ride away, but Heller wanted the last word.

"I'll give you a week to show me some more gold."

"Out of the question. It could take two or three, at least. Don't you understand? The mine is a mess. I have to go slow and easy or the damn thing might fall in on me. I might have to start an entire new hole. Then I have to haul out enough ore for an assay . . . By the way, is there an assay office in Pine Hollow?"

"No. Why would there be?"

"Then I'll have to go to Russell Junction, and

that'll take time. But if it doesn't test out at two thousand dollars a ton—"

"That doesn't sound like much."

"Twenty-five of your men can take out fifty to a hundred tons a day, if any of them can work, and if that mine is what I think it is."

"If," Heller said. Again Rocklin started away. "One more thing."

Rocklin didn't like the sound of it. Never in his experience had he wanted to get out of a place as much as he wanted to get out of Rathole, and as soon as possible. But Heller wanted to play with him a little more. He turned to face the man again. "Well?"

"You said you could have killed a dozen of my men when they were closing in on you. Ain't likely you meant with a gun, so I reckon you think you're pretty good with that knife you have stashed. Is that right?"

"I don't have time for this," Rocklin said impatiently.

"You got plenty of time, mister. Plenty." He took out his pigsticker. "I got a hankering to see just how good you are. Get down and get your blade out."

Rocklin dismounted. He was sneering. "Never mind my blade," he said. "I'll use yours." It stopped Heller for a second. "Come on, come on. What are you waiting for?"

Heller shifted his knife in his hand, holding it at his side, blade up. He went into a slight crouch.

Rocklin knew how to avoid a knife, but Heller had the reach on him as well as the height. It was

66

a weird kind of dance, with Heller swinging and thrusting, and Rocklin backing and weaving, but it didn't last long.

When Heller made just the right swing with his feet planted just the right way, Rocklin flipped him. He came down hard on his back, breathless and momentarily stunned. He shook his head, and became aware that Rocklin was over him with Heller's own knife pointed at his throat.

Bowdry stepped up, pulled the hammer back on his six-shooter, and pressed the muzzle to Rocklin's temple. Rocklin stood up and tossed Heller's knife in the dirt. Then he mounted the mule again and started away.

Heller got up and retrieved his knife. His men looked at him, and then at Rocklin's back. Heller didn't say anything. He hunkered down and watched Rocklin until he disappeared down the waterfall trail.

Nine

Heller tightened the watch on Rocklin. For a week there were riders on the prowl around the mine. They even made clearly visible camp at night, but they stayed outside the No Trespassing boundaries.

Rocklin had no choice but to keep busy. He chopped wood for no reason; he worked with a pick and shovel and wheelbarrow without accomplishing anything; he even placed dynamite and blasted, twice, thinking wryly that if he really wanted to make a farce of the whole routine, he could run out of the mine yelling, "Fire in the hole!"

Things didn't improve any when the weather kicked up. He had forgotten to check on the weather in the area—one more indication that he had rushed into the job under pressure. It had been years since he had spent any time in the mountains, and he had simply forgotten.

There were occasional thundershowers, and

once a real storm. Lightning set a forest fire just the other side of Granite Pass, and it burned two days before heavy rains doused it. There was a deep ravine that paralleled the south side of the pass and carried the Whitewater River down toward Pine Hollow. On the south side of the ravine were timbered slopes that stretched up toward high peaks. The fire blackened one of these slopes and laid a pall of smoke over the pass that stayed until the next storm moved in. And, to be convincing, Rocklin had to slosh around in the rain, hauling rocks out of the mine, and timbers in.

But he was able to do some useful things too. He fashioned a rough rock fireplace inside the tent for cooking and for warmth against the chilly nights. He widened the crosscut tunnel. He pounded together a crude ladder for the useless airshaft. He even chipped away at the top of it, trying to decide if it would take a dynamite charge. He badly needed a way up to the mesa that nobody else knew about. He had to slip in at night and take a thorough look around.

Finally, he decided to try placing a dynamite cap or two, and the results were encouraging. More water came through—it was dripping steadily now—but the structure held; he could work on it. He chiseled away at the top of the shaft until it was ready for one stick of dynamite. He set the charge with a slow-burning fuse and went out to the corral, pulling the animals to one side.

The blast brought some rock down, and with it some water. The water came down in a steamy flood at first, flowed almost to the mouth of the cave, and dwindled to a small stream. Rocklin went to investigate. He didn't expect what he found.

There was a man-size hole at the top of the shaft that clearly showed the sky. His first thought was, did they hear the blast in Rathole, and was it loud enough to make them curious? He was glad he had used a single stick of dynamite, because he had used four the two previous times, just for effect, and, with luck, the smaller blast, although virtually on top of the mesa, might not attract much attention. He would have to wait and see.

His second thought was, how old was the dump? For a dump—or part of a dump—was what came down with the water and the rock. There were old tin cans, disintegrating boots and other pieces of clothing, pots and pans that were almost completely rusted away, pieces of crude furniture, the rotted remains of a couple of straw ticks, even parts of an old horse pistol and a flintlock.

To Rocklin's relief, there was nothing that looked as if it had been thrown away recently, and he wondered how long there had been a camp or settlement of some kind on the mesa, and if it had gone back to the days of the mountain men.

The water was still coming down in a small but steady stream. Rocklin quickly cleared away the debris and positioned his ladder in the airshaft. it didn't take him very far, but he was near the top of the footholds he had chiseled, and he set to work making more. It was drudgery, and if it hadn't been for the small cracks and crevices left by the blast, it would have taken him the better part of the day to reach daylight. When he did, letting only the top of his head and his eyes show above the opening, he couldn't believe his luck. It was a very old dump, all right, and the stream that flowed through it had, over the years, cut a small crevice at an angle from the mesa down toward the face of the cliff. It was another, smaller, waterfall trail that had gone nowhere, because just below the dump the stream disappeared into a fault. Rocklin thought it was probably the same stream that came out of the side of the cliff beyond the corral.

Taking his time, Rocklin crawled up the streambed toward the mesa. The day was going, and by the time he reached the top, it was almost gone. He peered over the edge of the crevice, and through a cluster of juniper he could see a few dim lights in the distance. He had found another way up to Rathole.

On his way back down, he covered the top of the airshaft with an old piece of tin siding. He was soaked through and grimy when he got back to his tent, but he was satisfied.

Ten

Mary Tillman
17 Washington Square Place
New York City, New York

Dear Mary,

I may be getting ahead of myself, but I just might finish my part of this job and come home within the next week or ten days. Which is to say that the solution might be a lot simpler than anyone thought it was.

I will be glad to get home. I have been feeling vaguely unsettled ever since I left, and I have been aching to see you and the children, especially you.

It would be hard to imagine two worlds more different than this one and that one. I mean, the shelter, this camp and my own inner shelter, if that is not too high-sounding, is so flimsy, and there is such savagery all around. That sounds almost hypocritical in the circumstances, doesn't it? That,

I think, comes from trying to reconcile the irreconcilable, and I suppose I wouldn't be talking like this—I wouldn't even be thinking like this—if I were not sure of being home soon.

I shouldn't have taken the job. But having said that, have I said everything? I guess not. If you had said in words what you said by your manner—that you wished I were not going—would you have said everything? I don't know. I only know that I feel I owe you an apology. I must rely on you to tell me why.

I am glad you and I have always talked.

I hope you and the children are well.

You seem very close,
and I am as always
your loving husband,

William R. Tillman

Eleven

Rocklin had the uneasy feeling that he ought to be hurrying, something he never liked to do when he was on a job, and especially when he was in enemy territory, and strange enemy territory at that. But the night was heavy and damp, with clouds blotting out the moon and the stars. He had his compass and his pocket watch, and he had memorized the railroad's map of the area, but he was always aware that somewhere to his right as he circled the top of the mesa was the sheer cliff to the bottom.

When he first crawled out of the airshaft and recovered it with the sheet of tin, he had been aware that bad weather was on the way, and he was glad of it. He would have to be more careful of the terrain, but less careful of being spotted. Now, however, the barometer of his mind, sharpened by his years at sea, was dropping, and he faced the likelihood that he would not have all night to do what he needed to do. But he also knew he had to be *sure*. What it came down to was that he had to cut corners in such a careful way as not to miss what he was looking for.

He decided to head straight for the north point of the mesa, which was actually a little west of north, about 345 degrees on his compass. And at three miles an hour it would take him another two hours, if the weather and the darkness didn't slow him down too much.

He would bypass the whole northeast corner of the mesa, but from the reports he had read and his own observations, he was next to certain he wouldn't miss anything. Then he would follow the western rim all the way down to the south point, backtrack until he was clear of Rathole, and cut across to the airshaft. It was going to be rough, very rough when the weather slowed him down to one mile an hour or less, but with luck he would make it back to camp at first light. Simple.

The blackness deepened, and the wind was kicking up a fuss—head-on. He had to figure he was making less than two miles an hour now, but he maintained his pace deliberately so he wouldn't underestimate his progress. It wouldn't do at this stage of the game to walk off the edge of the damn rock.

Rocklin knew that no matter how dark the night, there was always some light to see by; it was there, in the atmosphere or somewhere. But when he suspected that he was near the edge of the mesa, he crawled; he had not come prepared for this weather.

The drizzle hadn't yet turned to rain, but that

was the only bright spot. He wondered if he should be turning back. He knew he could find the air-shaft again, with the help of his compass, his watch, and his sense of time, but then what? He would have to do it again. Besides, there was that nagging sense of urgency.

As it turned out, he knew he was at the edge before he felt it. It was there, yawning in front of him, empty space and a hundred-foot drop. By his reckoning, he should be able to see the lights of Russell Junction, about two miles away and a little bit east of north, but he could see nothing. He felt the edge, reached out with a stick he had picked up earlier and waved it at the void, picked up a rock bigger than his fist and gave it a little toss forward. He heard no sound of a rock hitting anything. He never did hear anything, except the wind.

He backed away fifty paces, got to his feet and started slowly south. He thought, all right, I won't be at the camp by dawn, but I'll use the weather as my cover.

An hour later, he saw the real storm coming, and in a way, it was welcome; lightning flashes to the northeast revealed the terrain below the mesa to him, an endless stretch of hills and evergreen forests. He was still close to the rim of the mesa, but he felt more sure of himself now. He walked faster. When he thought he was getting near the spot on the rim of the mesa where he could see something below, he moved closer and slowed down, making every step a careful one, like a blind man tapping the ground in front of each foot before he puts it down.

He stared into the blackness beneath him for a long time before he caught what he thought was a glimpse of light. It was back to the north. If it was what he had been looking for, he had overshot it by as much as a mile. Another glimpse. This time he was sure.

He started back, step by careful step, hoping the storm would hold off just a little while longer, trying to will it to hold off.

Suddenly, there it was. He could almost put his hand out and touch it—a crashing bolt of lightning so close to the timberline far below that there wasn't a split second between the light and the cracking roar of thunder that seemed to surround him. It was too close. The thunderhead would be here in a matter of seconds, and he was a standing target for lightning on top of a high mesa. He hit the ground and crawled for cover.

But the lightning flash had shown him the little gold town of Rand, as plain as day.

The worst of the storm raged for an hour, pouring rain and hail while Rocklin stayed down beneath the juniper in a cluster of rocks, using his slicker as shelter. He even managed to doze. He had slept during worse storms at sea when he was too exhausted to stay awake.

After the thunder and lightning and hail came the really hard rain. Rocklin had known he was in for more than a local squall, but the force of the rain surprised him. It came down like the waterfall, and it wasn't going to let up very soon.

Well, he couldn't stay here forever. He started to

make his way cautiously toward the edge of the mesa to take another look at Rand—if he could see it—and get his bearings, and he found himself tangled in the juniper.

The nap had disoriented him, and he had started out in the wrong direction. He felt for his compass and a match, crouched over to protect the light, and got a quick look before the light went out. He was facing north. He turned and tried to get out of the rocks and the bushes, but his way was blocked. He would have to feel his way along and get out the way he came in. It didn't take long, but it seemed like hours.

He was in the open again, and decided to check his compass. He crouched over and struck a match. Somebody said, "What the hell . . . Is that you, Lefty?"

It was so ridiculous, so unexpected, that Rocklin could only say, "Yeah," while he tried to decide which direction the voice came from. He didn't have a chance. A heavy body hit hard and slammed him to the ground. Apparently the lookout—for Rocklin was instantly aware that that was what he had to be—had concluded that it wasn't Lefty stumbling around in the dark and pouring rain.

The fight was a short one. Rocklin was able to lever his assailant off of him with an arm twist and a knee, but the man tackled him again, heedless of the mesa's rim. Either the lookout was very familiar with the lay of the land, or he had been as startled as Rocklin and had lost his head. Maybe he had tucked himself away in his storm shelter, and Rocklin had roused him. The man was like an angry animal.

Rocklin was not about to let the man hit him a third time—maybe he knew where the drop-off was and maybe he didn't—but the choice wasn't his. Grabbing wildly, the man took hold of Rocklin's slicker and whirled him around. Rocklin seized an arm, and felt a bone give as he made a desperate throw. He heard a squealing kind of cry fade into the blackness below as his own footing slid away and he went over the side.

Twelve

Something, a ledge, a tree, broke his fall. Then he was sliding, trying to flatten himself on a steep rock surface. Then he was being buried, smothered in what seemed like a mountain of mud. He tried to fight clear, but he was falling, and he was blacking out.

When he came to he was half-buried in the mud. In his slowly returning consciousness it took him a minute to remember where he was. He thought there were some dim lights, some shapes nearby. The ceaseless heavy rain was washing mud away from him. He lay absolutely still for awhile, cautiously testing each muscle and bone. He hurt. He was badly bruised and badly twisted. But he was sure nothing was broken. There *were* lights and shapes; he was practically in the town of Rand.

The cold was starting to penetrate to his core; he had to move. He hadn't moved three feet, half rolling and half crawling up and out of the mud, when he came upon the body of the lookout, head down and waist deep in the mire. They would figure he had lost his footing in the storm and gone over the cliff.

He didn't take much time for caution, thinking nobody would be out in this, and if they were, they wouldn't be able to see anything much. He had to get back to camp, and decide his next step.

The job was finished; his job, anyway. All he had to do was make his way to Fort Hatcher down on the flat east of Pine Hollow, wire Bannister, and tell him how many men were needed and where to send them. Bannister and the cavalry could do the rest.

He had done it the hard way, the only way open to him, but he had found the back door to the outlaw town of Rathole.

He had decided that first day, when he watched one man lead three horses with three bodies straight into the waterfall, that there had to be one. The waterfall trail was safe enough, and it wasn't easy to find, but no matter how closely it was watched, the outlaws would be finished if someone happened to stumble on it, as Rocklin did—and they had to know that. Why else had they tried so hard to drive him away?

All a posse or cavalry troop had to do was pull back into the trees and camp there, shoot any outlaw that came out of the waterfall from the single file trail, and starve out or freeze out the rest. No gang leader with the instincts of a hunted rabbit would put himself and his men in such a spot. So there was a back door.

Now all that was needed were two posses and two troops of cavalry. But they were needed quickly. If Dain Heller had the slightest suspicion that he could be trapped in Rathole, he would pull out. So Rocklin would head for the fort, and not trust to the railroad telegraph in Russell Junction. Heller no doubt had spies in the rail town.

But Buck was still at the mine; in the corral, safe enough, but with little food. And if Rocklin didn't show up . . .

It wouldn't matter a lot if the bad weather held; the outlaws probably wouldn't be watching too closely, and they wouldn't be expecting to see much work going on. But if some observant man noticed the absence of smoke from his tent . . .

All right. First, he had to go back. Load some rocks on the mule, and tell the sentries he was going into Russell Junction to have the ore assayed. Heller would send someone with him for sure, but that would be no problem. It would have to work. Second, he would have to avoid Russell Junction on his way back to the camp tonight, take the trail south from Rand, hit Granite Pass Road, and circle the southern end of the mesa from west to east. The distances were about the same, but he knew from the reports that the trail along the western face of the mesa was little-used and a lot rougher than the more frequently traveled roads going the other way. Third, should he steal a horse, or walk? He decided to walk; even a small thing like a missing horse could trip him up.

There was a fourth alternative, but a moment's thought told him it was not worth considering. If he tried to find the trail from the town to the back door of the mesa, he would be taking far too great a risk. He might not find it for hours. He would be spotted.

He made his way down the mountain of mud and cut the trail south.

Within a mile the trail turned sour. It was steep and rocky, and parts of it had been washed away. Rocklin started watching for any kind of shelter. It was two o'clock in the morning, and sunrise at this time of year was only four hours away. He wasn't going to make it, so he might as well stop for awhile, rest, and see how much blood he was losing from the various tears and scratches.

He tried to reconstruct his fall in his mind. The ledge he had hit wasn't far from the top of the mesa—he hadn't even felt anything but the jolt. Then there was brush growing from the side of the cliff. He had tried once, he was sure, to grab a handful, but he was falling too fast. Then there was a kind of slide, as though the cliff turned outward farther down. Then the mud. Where did the mud come from?

The rain had slacked off, and there was another thunderhead on the way. There were dim flashes of lightning in back of him, but the light reaching him was pale and diffuse. He hoped it would come closer and give him something to see by occasionally. The trail was straightening out some, and he went into an easy run.

There could have been a timber operation on the slope at the bottom of the cliff. He'had glimpsed one, in fact, when that sheet of lightning had shown him the town of Rand so vividly, and he had had the thought that it could be the source of Rathole's firewood. A stump-pulling operation could account for the fresh earth. Well, the thinking helped pass time.

His racing blood was warming him, and although running was painful, he felt better. He would have welcomed a lightning-set fire, but the rain was too heavy and had lasted too long. It did slack off for awhile, though, and he crawled into some heavy underbrush among the trees downhill from the trail, pulled his tattered slicker over him, and dozed for a spell.

The rain came back with a roar, and he woke with his teeth chattering. He climbed slowly back to the trail, every muscle aching and every bone creaking. There was lightning all around at a distance, and the light enabled him to work up to a fast walk, then a slow run. Soon he would be warm again.

He was thinking that with luck he might get back to the camp before light after all. Then his luck ran out. Twenty feet of the trail had crumbled away and was sliding down the hill toward the timberline. He almost stepped into the gap. But for a dim lightning flash, he would have. There was no way around it; he had to go down, and it took him an hour of crawling and climbing and feeling his way. It was hard work. Exhaustion and the altitude were beginning to tell. And the rain was not letting up; it seemed heavier.

It was a test of endurance now, a matter of slogging ahead regardless of exhaustion or pain, of detaching himself, simply checking out on the machine that kept him going, and knowing that the camp was there and he was going to reach it. Nothing, no thought, no aim, no circumstance could prevent it.

He couldn't see the lookout on the ledge through the rain, which meant the lookout couldn't see him. Good. He staggered on down Granite Pass Road toward the place where it emerged from the trees, planning to take to the forest and work his way to his camp without any chance of running into Heller's men.

To his right, south of the road, was the rugged gorge that carried the Whitewater River down to Pine Hollow, and on the opposite side of the gorge were the steep evergreen peaks, one of which had burned off a few days before. As he approached the cover of the trees that stretched in a line to form the eastern border of his camp, he became aware that the river was almost at the level of Granite Pass Road. It seemed impossible, but there it was. As near as he could make out, the gorge had been almost filled by rocks and mud and burned trees sliding down from the peak on the other side. The trees he could see—and by the depth of the slide, there must be hundreds—looked like so many used matchsticks in a jumbled and broken pile where the river used to be.

He heard something, and he stopped so suddenly he fell to his knees in the mud. It was a cry. At first he thought his battered body was playing tricks on him, but the cry came again. He tried to trace the sound through the pouring rain, but couldn't. He would have to circle around and search. It took him an endless and weary half hour to find them.

Thirteen

Huddled together under a dense clump of small trees just inside the timberline were four people, a man and a woman and two young people, a girl and a boy.

For a second, Rocklin could only stare. When the woman sat up and saw him, she said, "Thank God." It aroused the man and the boy, and the man put out his hand as though asking for help to get up.

"I thought I saw something through the rain," he said. "I yelled." The girl stirred, moaning softly. Her teeth were chattering so loudly that Rocklin could hear them through the relentless rain. He knelt and felt her cheek and neck. She was burning up.

"I have a camp near here," he told them, "but I've been away overnight. It will take me awhile to get a horse and a mule, and come after you. The girl should go with me."

"She can't move," the mother protested.

"I'll carry her. She's very sick. My guess is pneumonia. I can get her dry and warm. Then I'll come after you."

"No," the mother said. "She'll wait with us."

"I'll be back as soon as I can. About an hour." He started to turn away.

"Wait." It was the husband. He was trying to size up Rocklin. What he saw was a haggard and dirty man, unshaven and almost in rags. "How urgent do you think it is?" Rocklin was eyeing him. "You see, I've broken my ankle, or sprained it badly. I would be no good to you."

"It's urgent," Rocklin said. "Feel her face."

"I could go with you," the boy said.

Rocklin studied him. He was about sixteen years old, probably a couple of years younger than his sister. "Could you?" Rocklin asked.

The boy got up. "Yes sir."

"Come on then." Rocklin picked the girl up despite her weak protests and started for camp.

The mother cried out, and the husband tried to reassure her, but Rocklin and the boy were paying no attention. They were on their way.

The deep curtain of rain was as dark as ever, but Rocklin took the trail through the trees, just in case. The tent was tight and dry, and luckily Rocklin had stored firewood inside. He put the girl on his crude bunk and started stripping her of outer clothing.

"I'll help," the boy said tentatively.

"No need to take everything off," Rocklin told him. "Just the wettest of the outer clothing. Wrap her in blankets. I'll get a fire going. What's your name?"

"Richard Claude Legrande." Rocklin glanced at him. "My friends call me Dick." He was a sturdy, good-looking lad. Rocklin took to him.

"Well, Dick, as soon as you get her comfortable, start bringing in wood. There's plenty lying around outside, and we might as well get it all. We're going to need it."

"Is she going to be all right?" the boy asked.

"I don't know."

The fire was soon blazing, and Rocklin was heating some broth taken from a pot of cooked meat of various kinds that was a permanent fixture at the crude fireplace. The meat stock was quite fit to eat; it would nourish the girl and ease the chills. As it was coming to a boil, he gathered an extra sweater and jacket for the man and the woman, and added a couple of blankets. He knew they were already thoroughly wet and cold, and the trip would be fairly short, but the extra protection would reassure them.

"Heat a blanket and put it next to her," Rocklin said. "Then see that she drinks some of this soup. I'm going after your parents." He started through the double flap of the tent. "Oh. Stay inside until I get back."

The corral was dry, and there was grass left, but the animals were restless. Rocklin was as glad to see Buck as Buck was to see him. He saddled the horse, put a halter on the mule, and took an extra saddle blanket. As he was leading the animals away, he thought of one more thing. He went by the tent, took two buckets, went and filled them at the spring beyond the corral—a rushing stream now—and set them on the flat stones of the fireplace to heat.

"I'll be back soon," he told the youth, and was gone.

Richard Claude Legrande. There was a wealthy and well-known sportsman from Philadelphia whose name was John Claude Legrande. It was not beyond imagining that he had brought his family west on a hunting trip, and had fallen afoul of the unseasonable storm. And, Rocklin thought, the slide.

For the first time since he had found the stricken family, he thought of Rathole and Dain Heller—and of his plan, now shot to hell, for winding up the assignment and going home.

The first thing the woman said when Rocklin came with the wraps, was, "You left her alone?"

"No," he said shortly. "I left her with Dick."

"He's just a boy," she cried.

He tossed her the sweater and jacket. "Put these on. They'll make you feel better."

"Did you hear me?" she insisted.

The husband was struggling to his feet, holding onto a tree. Rocklin took an arm and put it around his own shoulder. "Can you get on the mule?" he asked.

"With a little help, yes."

"He's surefooted, and he leads well. We'll make it."

"How is Priscilla?" the wife asked.

"She's getting warm and Dick is feeding her some soup. You'll see for yourself soon."

When the man was mounted, Rocklin turned again to the woman. "You'll ride with me."

"I will not!"

Rocklin, bone-tired and impatient, picked her up and threw her onto Buck.

"John!" she appealed to her husband, but she stayed on. She knew about horses.

"Be quiet, Rose," her husband said gently.

Rocklin put a blanket around the woman's shoulders and climbed aboard Buck. Rose took hold of him gingerly, as though afraid of getting dirty. Nobody spoke during the ride to the mine.

The girl was delirious. She had a bad cough, very dry, and she kept trying in a weak way to throw her covers off.

Rocklin, as a ship's master, and later a rancher, had a working knowledge of the body and how to repair it, but he was no doctor. He had seen pneumonia before, though, and had done his best to treat it. He didn't think that fluid was reaching deep into the girl's lungs, but it was on its way unless he did something. He never went on a job without a medical kit as part of his gear, and one of the useful things he included was tincture of benzoin. It had helped a lot in healing and toughening his hands when he started working the mine. One of the first things he did when he reached camp with the parents was rig a tentlike canopy over the bunk, pour the benzoin into a pan of boiling water and put it under the covering for the girl to breathe. Later he would make a mustard plaster.

"Did she take any broth?" he asked Dick.

"Some. She's very hot."

"She has to stay warm. But it wouldn't hurt to bathe her face and forehead with some cool water. There's a spring coming out of the side of the mesa a little south of here. Dump the hot water in the washtub and go fill the buckets. There's a tunnel in back of the tent. It will take you to another mine entrance that's part corral. Go that way and turn south."

"Yes sir," Dick said.

"Are you all right? Are you warm enough?" Rocklin asked.

"Yes, thank you." He set about his chore.

Rocklin went to check the girl and pull the covers up.

"I'll do that," her mother snapped. She had been looking around the tent with her nose wrinkled as though the place smelled bad—and it probably did.

Rocklin stretched a rope across the tent near the back and threw a heavy blanket over it. "Wash off in here if you want to," he told her. "You should get out of those wet clothes."

"I am not a child, Mr.—"

"I'll look at that ankle as soon as I fix some soup," Rocklin said to the husband.

"It'll keep," the man replied. He watched Rocklin as he dipped some stock from the big

kettle, and cleaned and peeled some root vegetables from his meager supply. Rocklin had
brought only what would keep awhile—a few
potatoes, onions, rutabagas, carrots—nothing at
all fancy.

The mother added a little boiling water to the
pan with the benzoin.

"Our guide was killed in a landslide," Legrande
said. "We lost horses, supplies, everything. Our
tent was a little farther upstream. We just did make
it to safety before it was gone, too. We made it up to
the road before I fell and hurt my ankle, but the
rain . . ." He put his foot down the wrong way,
was reminded of his ankle, and started unlacing
his boot.

Dick came back with the water, and the mother
took a not-too-clean cloth that Rocklin handed
her, and set about cooling her daughter's face.

"What's in this mine, gold?" Dick asked.

"Not so far," Rocklin said.

"I like this place," the youth said. "It's a great
place for a camp, isn't it? Maybe I can explore a
little when the rain stops."

"You'll all have to stay in the tent until you're
ready to travel; then I'll take you into town."

The boy was too polite to ask why, but his face
showed that he sure wanted to. The father was
polite, too, but he had a responsibility.

"Are we in some kind of trouble, Mr.—"

Rocklin hesitated. He was busy gathering things
for a camp at the corral, but the hesitation was
unmistakable. "Rocklin," he said.

"My name is John Claude Legrande. To say I'm happy to meet you would seem redundant in the circumstances, wouldn't it?" Rocklin nodded. "We are in trouble, then?"

"You could be." Rocklin finished getting his gear together, and went to examine Legrande's ankle. "Can you wiggle your toes?" Legrande could. "Can you move your foot from side to side?" He could. "Does it feel like a broken bone when you do that?"

"It is painful, but no, it doesn't."

"I'll wrap it. You'll have to stay off of it for awhile."

Mrs. Legrande interceded. "I can do that, Mr., uh, Rocklin. What do you mean, we could be?"

"The girl should have a mustard plaster," Rocklin said.

"Do you have the ingredients? If you do, I can make it. Why could we be in trouble?"

"Yes, Mr. Rocklin, why?" Legrande said.

"There are people around here who would take you for ransom—sick or well, alive or dead."

"Don't be absurd!" Mrs. Legrande said. "That is a very cruel thing to say. A reliable guide led us up this way."

Dick was staring at Rocklin with what appeared to be great excitement. "Really? Do you really think so?" he asked.

Legrande was staring thoughtfully. "Then you know who we are?" he asked. He was far from stupid.

"I've heard of you. You may use any of the supplies that you find in camp. But don't show yourselves outside. Tomorrow I'll get a deer. I'll be in the corral; Dick knows how to get there. I'm going to sleep. Don't disturb me unless you have to."

"Thank you, Mr. Rocklin," Legrande said.

As Rocklin was going through the double flap at the back of the tent, Dick called, "I'll keep watch, Mr. Rocklin."

Fourteen

Rocklin slept for twenty hours. When he rolled out at six the next morning, the rain had stopped, but the sky was still overcast. And when he went back toward his tent by way of the tunnel, by-passed it, and stepped into the open air, Heller's watchdogs were there, just beyond the No Trespassing sign. He walked toward them carrying his rifle.

"I'm going after a deer," he said. "Later on I'm going into town for a few supplies. Anyone who dogs me when I'm after game runs the risk of being shot."

"Get your deer," one of the men said. "But I'll ride into town with you."

"Ride where you like, but keep your distance. I don't feel sociable."

"Do you ever?" the outlaw retorted.

The deer was no problem—Rocklin was back with it and had it dressed within two hours—but the family was, especially the mother.

"You *can't* go away and leave us," she insisted.

"The girl needs medicine. I have to go," Rocklin said.

Priscilla's fever was still high, but the tincture of benzoin and the mustard plaster were doing some good. Her cough was looser, and she was spitting up chunks of mucus.

"If her fever breaks, she'll be soaking wet," Rocklin said. "Don't let her throw the covers off."

"May I go with you?" Dick asked eagerly.

"No. Stay out of sight, all of you. If you go after water, Dick, go out the way you did before."

"Just how bad is it, Mr. Rocklin?" Legrande asked. "How sure are you that we haven't already been seen?"

"Pretty sure. The question is, how many people know that you are on a hunting trip in this area. How did you get here?"

"We came as far as Russell Junction in a private railroad car—a friend's. We tried to avoid being known, but . . ."

"But what?"

"Well, the guide knew my name. I can't know who, or how many, he told. He was highly recommended . . ."

"Was he a real guide? A good one?"

"Yes, he was."

"Then he probably didn't talk much. Good guides usually don't."

Dick couldn't contain himself. "Were those men you were talking to Western outlaws?" He asked.

Rocklin looked at Dick. "Yes. Now understand this, all of you. If those men thought there was profit in it, they would cut your throats without blinking an eye." He turned to Legrande. "You must not show yourselves. You may be safe here until the girl is strong enough to travel, but you must know that you'll be missed eventually. Eastern papers will report that the whole family is overdue from a hunting trip in wild country. Isn't that likely?" Legrande nodded slowly.

"The gossip will spread to Russell Junction and Pine Hollow faster than you can imagine. If you're lucky, searchers will assume you were buried in the avalanche. If they do, it will give you time. But if anyone gets wind of your presence here . . ." He let the warning hang.

"I understand," Legrande said.

"You're trying to frighten us," Mrs. Legrande said. "If what you say is true, how do we know you're not one of the cutthroats? Why are *you* here?" She was ignored, and her cheeks reddened.

"We can fight them off," Dick volunteered.

"It could come to that," Rocklin said. He turned again to Legrande. "Is there any chance at all that your guide led you in this direction for reasons of his own?"

"No. None. You see, I was in this area years ago as a young man, with a Union patrol during the Civil War. We were escorting a gold shipment to the East. I always remembered the mesa. I thought it was one of the most wild and beautiful spots I had ever seen. We were trying to lose a rebel force that had found our trail, and we camped on top of it. Everyone now says there is no way up; even our guide said so; but I know there is.

"And I got my family into this, may God forgive me, because I thought it would be a fairly easy trek from Russell Junction to Pine Hollow if we followed the Whitewater River around the mesa. I *knew* I would recognize the trail if I ever saw it. On the way up there was a beautiful little lake, and on the way down there was a waterfall. But it was all different . . . Believe me, Mr. Rocklin, we've been on tougher treks than this."

"Not quite," Rocklin told him. "The top of the mesa is where the outlaws hole up. In fact, the place is called Rathole. Did you ever hear the name mentioned?"

Legrande shook his head. He had gone white around the lips. He was a courageous man, but his family was involved now.

"I did," Dick said. He was almost shouting in his excitement. "I heard some boys in town talking about it. And then I was talking to our guide, and he said it was a place to stay clear of. Father wanted to go where the Bighorn sheep were, and—"

"You'll have to keep your voices down when I'm gone," Rocklin warned. "This camp will be watched all the time. I don't think anyone will approach, but if they do, Dick will lead the way through the tunnel. You'll have to make it somehow. Pile some rocks and tools in front of the tunnel entrance as you go through. If anyone comes, they won't be curious enough to follow . . ."

"Are you sure this is the best way, Mr. Rocklin?" Legrande asked.

"No. But I am sure that the most urgent thing is

food and medicine . . ." He was interrupted by a thought. If he could get the cavalry, now, tonight . . .

"What?" Legrande asked. "What were you thinking?"

How long would it take? The road to Pine Hollow would be treacherous, and the rain wasn't over, by any means. The ride across the flatland to the fort wouldn't be bad, but he had never been over the road to Pine Hollow.

He could tell Heller's spies that he would stay overnight in Pine Hollow if it started pouring rain again . . .

"I was thinking about how likely it is that your name is already known in Russell Junction and Pine Hollow, and if there is talk that your party is lost in the storm."

Legrande thought about it and said, "I simply couldn't guess. What do you think?"

Rocklin said, "I think it likely enough that we have to assume it, to be on the safe side."

"And?"

Dick's mind was running on one track. "You have lots of guns. We could hold them off until you got back!"

"You're in enough trouble without borrowing any," Rocklin told him. He turned to Legrande. "I don't have to tell you how important it is that you lie low." Legrande nodded, waiting for him to go on. "I can get a troop of cavalry up here, but not until tomorrow morning at the earliest. There's a fort ten miles east of Pine Hollow. It will take time, and it will be risky, because it will show our

103

hand. The question is, would it be better to hide, keep your presence here secret, until the girl is well enough to travel, and, maybe, until the weather clears."

"I see," Legrande said. He was a careful man, too. He thought about it. Then he asked a question. "Cavalry troops will move on your say-so, Mr. Rocklin?"

Now it was Rocklin's turn to consider. But not for long. "Yes," he said.

"I see. It's quite a choice, isn't it?" He thought some more. "Tell me, is the waterfall still there?"

"It is. Not more than half a mile from here."

"As I remember it, one good man could keep them from escaping that way."

"That's right. But there's the other way. It's still there, too. But there's a mining operation right at the bottom of it, or very close. There's no way you could have recognized it."

"Ah. Of course. We didn't go near it. We followed the river. But I could see it clearly. So you need two troops of cavalry?"

"Exactly."

"So that's the reason . . . Tell me, how long have you known about the two accesses?"

"Since night before last."

Legrande nodded. "And then we came along and . . . You would have been gone today, wouldn't you?"

"Or I would be thinking it over."

"We can't move Priscilla until she's ready," Rose Legrande said.

"So, if you went after the cavalry tonight, *we*

could be safer, but your plans could go awry?" Legrande said.

"Maybe. On both counts. But only maybe," Rocklin said.

"Will there be a great risk for you in just going into town for food and medicine?"

"There is always risk," Rocklin replied.

"Then the decision is yours," Legrande said.

"I won't know for sure what I'll decide until I get into town," Rocklin told him.

"I understand. Good luck, Mr. Rocklin."

Rocklin started to leave.

"Mr. Rocklin." It was Rose Legrande. "Be careful."

Rocklin looked at her for a brief moment. It occurred to him that she was a very attractive woman. He turned and left.

Fifteen

Something was going on in the ravine below the pass.

Rocklin wanted to know, but since his tail was only fifty yards behind him on Granite Pass Road, he did not want to step out of character by appearing too curious. He was still the cranky miner who was only interested in gold and just wanted to be left alone. But he could stop and look for a minute.

The landslide had made a crude dam across the Whitewater River, and the rushing water was very high in back of the dam. But already the river was cutting a channel through the mud and debris, eating away at the slide. Tons of mud, rocks, and small trees were breaking away and hurtling downstream in the foaming water.

There was clearly trouble downstream, because men were working around the dam with axes and saws and peaveys, trying to place heavy logs and rocks to reinforce the mud pile and make it more stable so it wouldn't let go all at once and sweep away anything below it, possibly including the town of Pine Hollow. Some of the men appeared to be wearing cavalry boots and pants.

It set Rocklin to wondering just how much trouble there was along the river, and how many horse soldiers were left at the fort. He glanced back at the man dogging him and saw that he, too, was watching the activity at the river. He tried to spot the sentry on the ledge, but the drizzle had started again and it was too thick. In fact, Heller had ordered no more lookouts on the ledge until the soldiers left.

Rocklin was thinking about Heller as he nudged the mule down the road, wondering how edgy he was getting, having the Army so close to his hidden outlaw trail. If the results of the storm, which wasn't over yet, made it necessary for the gang to stay in its hole, there was time . . .

Pine Hollow surprised Rocklin. It was well situated on the river, with the forest behind it and the plain stretched out in front of it. Basically, it was a cattle town, an adjunct to Big Jim Haggard's ranch, but Rocklin could see that it was unusually neat and well kept. Now, however, the southern side of it—a seedy section of scattered saloons, shacks, and cribs beyond the river—was stuck in two or three feet of water and mud. Townspeople, cowhands, and more troopers from the fort were working to raise both banks of the river with rocks, logs, and sandbags.

A few men were hanging around the saloon, some looking as if they had been there all day, some grimy and tired. There were three muddy troopers at the bar, minding their own business.

Rocklin asked for whiskey, and the bartender put a bottle in front of him. He was about to toss it down when his tail came through the front doors. He turned away, caught the man's image in the glass behind the bar, and saw him look around the room, catch someone's eye, and nod slightly in his direction. Then the outlaw went farther down toward the end of the bar, ignoring Rocklin.

"Is there a doc in town?" Rocklin asked the bartender. He looked as if he could use one. He was bruised and scarred, and he was wearing the same clothes he had worn to the mesa, and they were ragged and dirty.

"A frame house just in back of the store," the barman said. "Looks like you need one."

"A little cave-in," Rocklin muttered. He saw the young agent from the railroad come in the doors with a man who was undoubtedly Deputy Big Nose Homer Slate. He paid no attention. Someone at the back of the room got up and joined the deputy and the agent at the bar, saying something to them that no one else could hear. Big Nose and the agent looked at Rocklin, and then the sheriff signaled with a jerk of his head for the barman to join them, and talked to him briefly. He finished his drink and moved down the bar toward Rocklin.

"I'm Homer Slate, deputy sheriff in Pine Hollow. Are you the crazy miner people are talking about?"

Rocklin glared at him. "I'm prospecting. What's it to you?"

Big Nose said genially, "Oh, nothing. Nothing."

"Which way's the store?" Rocklin asked the barman, who pointed toward the river.

"Don't get into any trouble, miner," Big Nose said, but Rocklin was on his way. As he left the saloon, the hardcase who had followed him, and another man, took up the tail.

The doctor, a friendly and loquacious man, told him more than he wanted to know about the flood, but less than he wanted to know about the town. Talkative but careful. Rocklin revealed no curiosity about anything; he just wanted some advice about a persistent cough, and some medicine. The doctor gave him some castor oil and a bottle of brilliant red liquid that Rocklin suspected was half alcohol. Well, even if it didn't help clear the girl's bronchial tubes, it might make things seem rosier.

Rocklin put off buying supplies in favor of a few hours of sleep, but he woke up in the middle of the night with his mind made up to leave for the fort, right then.

He slipped out the back door of the two-story hotel and made his careful way toward the trail east. There was still weary activity at the river, men working by the light of coal oil lanterns and carbide lamps, but otherwise the town was quiet. It made it easy for him to spot his tail.

There was no help for it. Rocklin knew he couldn't have anyone reporting to Heller that he had been sneaking around in the night. He waited in the shadow of an alley for the man, killed him quickly and silently, and robbed him, later throwing the loot in the river. He stole an Army horse, walked it out of town, and headed east at a gallop.

He planned to get back to his hotel bed at least an hour before dawn, and if Big Nose was curious about the dead man, he would find that Rocklin had been asleep, and his mule had been in the livery stable all night.

Colonel Race, the commander at the fort, was an old-timer, tall and wiry, patient and unruffled, despite being turned out by a scruffy-looking civilian riding an Army horse who wouldn't take no for an answer from a suspicious corporal of the guard.

When the corporal left, Rocklin said, "I'm sorry, Colonel, but I need to use your telegraph. My name's Rocklin."

"Rocklin. Rocklin, yes. I received urgent orders some time ago from Washington—coded, I might add—to see that you got anything you asked for. I take it that somebody has finally decided that something had to be done about the Heller gang."

Rocklin didn't hesitate. "That's right. But I hope no one but you knows about it."

"Everybody knows about the gang, but nobody knows about my orders." He opened the door to his office and told a sleepy orderly, who was still pulling on his clothes, "Get the telegrapher."

It took awhile for the wire to Bannister to be

sent, because Rocklin had to encode it.

LEGRANDE PARTY IN MY CAMP. ILL-NESS PREVENTS FURTHER MOVEMENT. BECAUSE OF STORM THEY MAY BE SAFE FOR FOUR OF FIVE DAYS. NO LONGER. TWO WAYS INTO RATHOLE. GANG CAN BE BOTTLED UP AND STARVED OUT WITH HELP OF TROOPERS. EXPECT FULL COOPERATION FROM EVERYONE CONCERNED. R.

When Rocklin told Race what he wanted, the colonel said, "I'm sorry, Rocklin. I have no men at the moment."

"What?"

"There is only a small security force here. Twenty-four of my men are at the Whitewater River in Pine Hollow and at the pass, and twenty-four are at Rand. The rest are at least twelve days south of here by forced march. Bandits have been raiding across the border again, and Fort Apache asked for help."

Rocklin didn't waste time ranting and cussing. He considered the problem while the colonel sat quietly, waiting.

"Who's in charge?" Rocklin asked.

"Lieutenant Schroeder at Pine Hollow and Lieutenant Gunning at Rand. Gunning is here now, but he'll leave again at dawn. Do you want to talk to him?"

"I would appreciate it."

Race yelled for the orderly and told him to go get Gunning, and when the lieutenant arrived, told him to answer Rocklin's questions.

For an hour, Rocklin questioned the officer about every detail of the town of Rand, and about the temporary dams they were helping to build above it to hold back the river until it subsided. The officer showed some insight. His answers were precise and to the point, but he didn't hesitate to volunteer information if he thought it might be useful.

"You've been in the town before, then," Rocklin said.

"Several times. When the mine was in top production . . ." he glanced at the colonel, who nodded for him to go ahead, ". . . we occasionally escorted large shipments of gold to the railroad at Russell Junction."

"The mine isn't at full production now?" Rocklin asked.

Again Gunning hesitated, and again Race nodded. "It hasn't seemed to be producing much for some time," he said.

"Do you mean they're keeping up appearances?"

"It looks that way to me."

"Tell me," Rocklin said, "do you see many hardcases hanging around town, men who don't seem to have any reason to be there?"

"No." Gunning thought for a minute. "Except for the guards."

"At the mine," Rocklin said.

"Yes. Actually . . ."

"Yes?" Rocklin prodded.

"Actually, since we've been at the river, I've wondered if they might be part of the Heller gang. They don't help. They don't do much of anything but hang around the saloon."

"That's the place just north of town?" Rocklin asked.

"Yes. When some of my men first showed up there, the guards acted like it was their private territory, tried to pick fights, things like that."

"But they don't anymore?"

"No. They're even . . . unobtrusive, you might say."

"As if under orders?" Rocklin asked.

"Yes."

Silence. Rocklin was taking time to think about all he had been told. Finally, he said, "Lieutenant, I would like you to go back over in your mind everything you know about Rand. Get a clear picture of it. Think about it. And then tell me this: If there's a trail from the top of the mesa that comes out somewhere in Rand, where does it come out?"

Gunning looked doubtful, but he did what he was asked. He closed his eyes and studied the scene in his mind for several minutes. He was shaking his head slowly. "You're saying there is a way to the top of the mesa," he said at last.

"Yes. Where does it come out?"

"Do you mean Rathole is up there?"

"Yes."

"I've been around that mesa five times. All the way. I can't believe it. Pardon me for asking, but how do you know?"

"Stick to the question, Lieutenant," Race ordered.

"It's all right," Rocklin said. "I'm going to have to give you the whole picture, anyway. But it absolutely goes no further. Understood?" The two men nodded. "You know the waterfall?"

"Of course," Gunning said.

"That's one way. The trail, an old watercourse, starts behind the fall, but only one man on a horse can go up or down at a time. I've been up it." Both the lieutenant and the colonel were staring at Rocklin in disbelief. "And I know the north trail comes out onto the mesa just above Rand, but the bottom of it must be pretty well hidden, and somewhere in the town. It has to be. I ran into the lookout up there."

"The lookout?" the colonel echoed.

"A man was found dead . . ." the lieutenant began.

"That was the lookout," Rocklin said. "But I couldn't see anything up there but a few lights. I was right on top of the town, but the storm was right on top of me . . ."

"But how did you get down?" the lieutenant blurted.

"I fell."

The colonel exploded. "I don't believe it!" Rocklin didn't say anything. "I don't mean I don't believe *you*. I mean I don't believe *it*. They've been up there all the time?"

"Yes. And my question is, how do they get up there from the town? What about the saloon?"

"The saloon?"

"Yes, Lieutenant, the saloon. As you described it, it's right up against the bluff."

"That's right."

"What's in back of it?"

"I don't know. Nothing. Well, an outhouse, I suppose. There's a burlap curtain into a back room, just a storage room, from the glimpses I've gotten of it, and then another door . . . well, there has to be an outhouse . . ."

"All right, here's the situation," Rocklin said. "We can't risk letting Heller know we're on to him. He would run for it, if he could, and fight his way out. He couldn't do that at the waterfall trail, but he might do it at Rand. I don't know for sure.

"The weather is on our side; nobody's going to go out in it unless he has to. So all I need is four or five men to keep an eye on the waterfall trail. The men working at the landslide can bivouac just inside the tree line, and their breaks can be rotated so that there are four or five of them in the camp at all times." He was talking to both men now, and they were listening carefully.

"Now this is important: If anyone comes out of the waterfall and starts down the road to Pine Hollow—and it's unlikely that anyone will be heading over the pass—your men will have to let him get out of sight of the fall before they take him." He turned to Gunning. "Do you know the rocky ledge just below the pass?"

"Yes."

"Heller has a sentry on it at all times. He can't see much in this weather, but your men have to be careful. They should be handpicked."

116

"They will be," Colonel Race assured him.

"I will have more men in a few days, if I can impose on your telegrapher again."

The colonel smiled. "My orders are to give you anything you want." The lieutenant glanced at his commanding officer in astonishment.

"My men will be in Army uniforms, to make them less conspicuous, and will report to Schroeder in Pine Hollow. Is he reliable?"

"Completely," Race replied.

"The point is," Rocklin went on, "that we have to plug both escape routes before Heller knows what's going on, and starve them out or freeze them out. They have very little firewood up there, and my guess is that the weather has caught them off guard.

"Rand is another matter, though," Rocklin said. "For all I know, they can storm down that trail. We'll have to close the town completely."

"Without arousing suspicion?" Gunning asked. "How?"

"Isn't the river overflowing into privies?" Rocklin asked.

"Not so far."

"Yes, it is. Sewage is showing up in the river. One of your troopers has caught typhoid. You're going to have to quarantine the town."

Gunning looked at the colonel, who said, "It should work. It's certainly believable. In fact, I've been concerned about it."

"What about Schroeder?" Rocklin asked.

"He's due in today," Race said. "Gunning and I will brief him." He paused before asking, "What will you be doing?"

"Taking care of a problem at the mine," Rocklin said.

He wasn't sure why he said it. Of course, everyone had heard of the crazy miner, and the colonel had taken it for granted that Rocklin was the man. That was why he hadn't even asked Rocklin who he was; he hadn't seen the point in belaboring the obvious. And for some reason, Rocklin felt like letting the colonel know that his assumption was correct.

Race accepted Rocklin's answer. He nodded briefly and yelled for his orderly to fetch the telegrapher.

"Rand, by the way, is a company town," Rocklin said.

Race nodded, and said the rest for him. "And Jim Haggard owns it. And yes, I know Haggard. I've exchanged dinner invitations with him. After all, he's the most powerful man in this area."

Rocklin hesitated, then said, "The reason I don't want to use any of Haggard's riders—"

The colonel stopped Rocklin with a gesture. "I have assured you of my complete cooperation, Mr. Rocklin. That includes my discretion." He smiled, and added, "Of course, you'll return the Army horse."

"Of course," Rocklin said. "But I'm afraid I can't thank the trooper who loaned him to me."

Pine Hollow was very dark and quiet, except for the work at the river. Rocklin put the horse back where he got it and wiped it down, eliminating the possibility that some trooper would say, "Hey, who's had my jughead out!" He checked the signs he had carefully placed at the window and door of his room, found they hadn't been disturbed, and turned in.

He was awakened an hour later by a pounding on his door. It was Big Nose Slate, who didn't waste any words. "The rider who came into town just after you did?"

"You mean Heller's watchdog?" Rocklin asked. The answer was not quite what the sheriff had expected. His genial pose vanished; his eyes narrowed, and he put his hand on his gun. Rocklin just looked sleepy. "He's dead," the sheriff said. "Murdered."

"Well, that's no great loss to me. No gain either. He wasn't bothering me. Is that all?"

"I'm going to have to hold you a couple of days, while I look into it."

"Without checking with Heller?" Rocklin asked. He was fully alert now, and reaching for his clothes, where his knife was hidden. The sheriff's reaction was almost comical. He wanted in the worst way to pull his gun and shoot Rocklin dead, but he was controlling the lethal impulse through fear. The look on his face was something to see, and his big nose twitched in his agitation. "Haven't you heard?" Rocklin asked. "We're partners in a mining enterprise."

Slate was speechless. He turned and made a good try at storming out of the small room.

Rocklin didn't waste any time. With the sick girl in mind, he did the best he could at buying supplies, considering the limited stock at the general store. He picked a dozen eggs, at a dollar apiece, some flour from a weevil-infested barrel—it didn't bother him, weevils and flour were a natural combination at sea—sorghum, coffee, some extra blankets, a new oilskin slicker, and lots of soap.

The store was filled with curious people, whispering, watching him with sidelong glances.

While he was tying his supplies on the mule, the people found a new reason for exciting gossip. Three bodies, a man and two horses, had been found in the landslide below Granite Pass. There were rumors of a missing hunting party, a rich family from back East who came into Russell Junction in a private railroad car. The men at the slide were looking for more bodies. Rocklin didn't have any apparent interest in any of it. He paid for his supplies and left.

Another of Heller's men followed him clear back to the No Trespassing sign at the mine, and Rocklin was relieved to see that there was little or no smoke coming from his camp, despite the persistent rain, which had ranged from a drizzle to a downpour during his entire trip.

Sixteen

There were embers in the fireplace, and the tent was warm. The first thing Rocklin did was restrain Dick from going out and taking care of the mule, reminding him that he had to stay out of sight. The next thing was to check on the girl. She was sleeping soundly.

"Her fever broke about an hour ago," Rose Legrande told him. "She's been like that ever since."

Rocklin glanced at the dying fire. "Has she been warm enough?"

"We built up the fire at night," Legrande told him, "and heated some rocks to put next to her in the daytime. We've been very careful."

"It's stifling in here most of the time," Rose Legrande said.

"I'll open everything up, front and back," Rocklin said. "We'll get a good blaze going." Dick went immediately to work. "There's another storm on the way," Rocklin told them. "That's in

121

our favor. They've found the body of your guide and two of your horses at the landslide, so it's only a matter of time until they discover that you weren't killed. There's talk already; your names will be known any day.

"There aren't many troops available right now because of flood-control work and bandit raids down at the border," he told Legrande, "but both escape routes from the mesa are being sealed off. All we have to do now is wait until your daughter is able to make the trip into town."

The camp settled into a routine of sorts. Rocklin slept in the cave at the corral, and the Legrandes made do with the tent. Laundry was kept at a minimum because of the wetness, but what had to be done, Priscilla's clothes and blankets and such, was done in the space in back of the tent and dried on a line stretched in front of the fireplace. Legrande had fashioned a crude crutch from some small limbs, and did most of the light work, including the cooking, and Dick and Rocklin carried water from the rushing spring.

One day, Rocklin saw Dick and Rose Legrande trying to manage the washtub, filled with fresh water, between them, and carrying buckets in their free hands. "That's not necessary," he said to the woman, taking her bucket and the tub handle. She looked tired.

She wanted to say something, but didn't seem to know how to start. "Mr. Rocklin . . ."

Rocklin glanced back at her, but he and Dick were maneuvering the tub through the crosscut tunnel.

"I . . . We don't know how to start to thank you . . ."

"Not necessary," he said. "We still have to get out of here."

Her expression showed that she took it as a rebuff. He wanted to apologize for his abruptness, but he was occupied and the moment passed.

Rocklin disposed of his tattered clothes, bathed in the rain at the spring, and trimmed his beard to keep up appearances. He also kept up his pretense of mining when he had time, even doing some blasting.

He spent as little time as he could at the tent. He took his meals there because it seemed both a waste of time and churlish not to, but otherwise he tried to busy himself elsewhere.

When he was in the tent, the girl's eyes followed his every movement, and her mother was uneasily aware of it.

The second night after Rocklin had returned from town, when he had finished eating and started out of the tent, the girl said, "Why didn't you just leave us?"

The question caught everyone's attention. The mother, startled, looked at the girl, ready to remonstrate, then changed her mind and looked at Rocklin.

Rocklin stopped and glared at the girl. "Nonsense," he said, and started again to leave.

"That's a funny way for a dirty miner to talk," Priscilla said. "My brother says you're an important government agent sent out from Washington."

"Your brother is a fine boy, but he dramatizes things."

"Maybe. But since you saved our lives, you owe us something. You can't just save a person's life and let it go at that. It's too earth-shattering. It seems to me that it would leave you deeply committed."

Rocklin was looking down at her. "It's an interesting way to look at it. Some societies do look at it that way. I'll bet you read a lot."

The girl looked offended. "It was my own idea," she said.

"I apologize," Rocklin said. "A girl should value her own ideas."

"I'm a young woman," she said, offended again.

"I apologize again," Rocklin said, and left.

"Good night, Mr. Rocklin," Dick called out.

The strain began to tell on everyone, but especially on Rose Legrande. Rocklin tried to avoid her, but she seemed to go out of her way to complain and pick quarrels with him.

The first was about the weevils. He had shown her how to make pan bread, and she had wrinkled her pretty nose at the flour Rocklin had brought from Pine Hollow. Later she sought him out at the cave behind the corral and said she simply couldn't use flour with bugs in it.

"The bugs don't hurt anything," Rocklin said, "and the bread is nourishing. You don't have to eat them. Pick them out before you bite into the bread."

"You can't be serious."

"I'm busy, Mrs. Legrande."

"Doing what? You yourself admit this isn't really a mine. Why do you go to the trouble? You don't actually think it does any good, do you?"

"No. I only hope it does. If it keeps them wondering a few days longer, it will be worth it."

"Then you'll be rid of us."

"Yes."

She was furious.

Later, when Rocklin set off dynamite, she came back. "Is there any real need for that horrible noise, Mr. Rocklin? Or are you just seeing how objectionable you can be?"

He was swinging a pick at the loosened rock at the back of the cave, and pulling it out onto the floor. When he finally spoke, he was prying a fairly large chunk loose, and he said, "Watch yourself."

She didn't move, and as she watched him load the wheelbarrow and push it out through the rain to dump it beyond the rail fence, she was at her most disdainful.

Dick showed up, as usual after a blast, and said, "I'll help," and grabbed a shovel. "Mr. Rocklin's going to show me how to set a dynamite charge," he told his mother.

"He certainly is not," Rose Legrande said. "Mr. Rocklin, you couldn't possibly agree to such a thing without asking me first."

"I asked Dad," Dick said brightly.

"I'll see about this," she said, and left. Rocklin heard no more about it.

The next morning at breakfast she said, "Mr. Rocklin, the blankets are full of bugs."

125

"Shake them out," he said. "The bugs won't bother you if you bathe and wash your hair in some of that strong lye soap."

She was horrified. Legrande, who had never been able to deny his wife anything, pretended that he was not aware of the conflict. His expression was bland.

After Rocklin returned to his cave, she came by with two large buckets on her way to the spring. She was struggling with them on her way back, pointedly ignoring him, when he stopped what he was doing and said, "You don't have to do that." She put the buckets down and glared at him—in a ladylike way. "But if you insist, why don't you fill up at the airshaft. The water is from the same stream—a little dirtier because a lot of it's rainwater and it isn't filtered through rock. But you boil it anyway."

She didn't answer. She left the buckets of water where they were and left through the crosscut.

The water had been coming down the airshaft since the heavy rain started, and there was now a small but steady stream running handily through Rocklin's camp. The camp smelled of wet burning wood and horse manure, but it was a cozy odor compared to that in the tent. Rocklin picked up the buckets, carried them to the tent, and poured them into the tub that was always heating at the fireplace.

The real blowup came that afternoon when Rocklin was leaving the tent and saw Rose Legrande walking toward the mine entrance with a bucket of dirty washwater. He caught her just as she was throwing it out, took her firmly by an arm, and pulled her back behind the protective log wall. He said, "If you do that again, I'll shake your teeth loose."

"How dare you!" She almost spit it out.

"I dare because I intend to get you out of here with a whole skin. I'll say it for the last time. Stay away from the front of this camp. There are men watching."

"You are the most arbitrary, crude, brutal man I've ever known," she said. "I believe the outlaws would be preferable to you."

"Keep acting the fool and you may get a chance to test that belief," Rocklin said. Later, as he passed the tent, he heard Legrande talking to his wife in a low but far from gentle voice.

Still later, she intercepted him when he was on his way to supper. "Mr. Rocklin," she began in a low voice, "I . . . I owe you an apology. I have been behaving abominably, and I . . ." She was having a hard time of it, but Rocklin was in no frame of mind to help. "There's no way to tell you how much I . . . how grateful . . . how much we owe you."

"Don't tell me," Rocklin said. "I don't want to hear it. You hate being beholden to anyone, Mrs. Legrande, and you have too much pride for gratitude, which is part of *civilized* behavior."

Rocklin didn't go in to dinner. He built up the fire in his cave and ate a can of pork and beans.

The new storm was in full fury, and no one at

Pine Hollow or Rand thought anything of it when more troops started coming in. Some of them camped at the timberline just below the lookout ledge at Granite Pass.

The development was reported to Heller, and he went into a rage. The weather was getting to him, and everything sent him into a rage. "It's that damn miner. He's bringing them in," he yelled.

"It's the storm," Hank Bowdry said. "They're trying to keep the towns from washing away."

"It's both, I tell you. He's boxing us in."

"Boxing us in? What do you mean?"

"I mean the troops in Rand! What's the matter with you, Hank? You ain't keeping up."

"They're trying to hold back the river in Rand. You can't blame the miner for that."

"Yeah? What happened to the man you had posted at the trail?"

"What?"

"He's dead, ain't he?"

"He lost his footing during the storm and fell," Bowdry said. He was being patient, which made Heller even angrier.

"The miner killed him!"

Bowdry was flabbergasted. It occurred to him that Heller was afraid. He had never seen that before, and he couldn't believe it. The man didn't have the human feelings to be afraid. He was acting like a trapped animal, and it was mostly in his head.

"Let me ask you something, Dain," he said. "Why did you let him ride down out of here?"

"Because he's too tricky not to have an ace up his

sleeve, that's why. Do you think he would have come up here if he didn't? I got to find out what it is. What did he do in town? I'll tell you what he did. He went out to the fort. That's why he had to kill Jake, to get him off his trail.''

"There's no sign that he went anywhere but to bed,'' Bowdry argued. "His mule never left the stable.''

"Then he stole a horse! He got out there somehow.''

"Nobody reported a stolen horse,'' Bowdry pointed out. "If he's got us trapped, why doesn't he just go home and leave it to the Army?''

"I don't know! All I know is there's a reason.'' He had a thought. "Have any more bodies shown up at the slide?''

"No. Just three more horses.''

"Why didn't you tell me! Where's the hunting party, then?''

Bowdry thought about this. "You don't mean the miner has them?''

"Why not?''

"It doesn't make sense. If he's as smart as you think he is, what's he doing with a tenderfoot family? Holding them for ransom?''

"What do you mean, ransom? What about the family? Who are they?''

"I wasn't serious. Their names are Grand, or something like that. Swifty told me that the paper in Russell Junction called the old man a million-aire sportsman.''

"Why didn't I know about that?'' Heller raged. "I've told everyone a hundred times that I got to know everything. Everything, dammit!"

"It's all been mostly guesswork up to now, Dain."

"I'm tired of guesses. I need the straight of it, not guesses. That family's *somewhere!* I want more men watching that mine. If that sidewinder has got them, I want to know it. Hell, they were camping right below that slide, weren't they?"

"As far as anyone knows."

"Then maybe they're hurt. Maybe they can't travel. Git in there. One way or another, git in there and find out. Watch for him to drop his guard, and kill that miner. Maybe he's got a million dollars in that phony mine, after all."

The thought hadn't occurred to Bowdry. There wasn't much he hadn't done while riding with Heller, but his crimes hadn't included kidnapping.

"I'll make sure. But I think you're barking up the wrong tree, Dain."

Seventeen

A slight sound brought Rocklin instantly awake.

It was the third night after his return from Pine Hollow, and the rain, the dragging time, and his anxiety about Heller's next move were making him restless. He was wondering if the sound was part of a dream, when it came again. Someone was coming through the tunnel.

He extracted himself silently from his bedroll, slipped on his boots—all he needed to be fully dressed—took his knife out, and waited just outside the tunnel. The remains of his fire offered a weak light, and the dark figure that emerged from the tunnel cast a dim shadow on the stone. It was Dick. Something was wrong.

"What is it, Dick?" he whispered.

"I heard something," the boy said. "Just outside the tent."

"What did it sound like?"

"Someone's out there."

"Stay here," Rocklin told him. "Don't leave until I come and get you."

"I could help."

"You already have. First, I have to find out what we're up against."

"I did hear something." The boy was emphatic.

"I believe you. Stay here."

Rocklin went out into the rain. The sound of it, and the limited visibility made it necessary for him to circle carefully around and sneak up on the tent. He went as fast as he could directly toward it.

Someone was outside, all right. At least four of them as far as he could tell from the sounds. Rocklin was about to run into one of them when the man heard or sensed something and whirled to face him. Rocklin's knife stopped the sound in his throat.

It was too close. Rocklin slowed down a little. When he located the next man, he was only four paces away, and Rocklin killed him so quickly the man never knew what happened. The third man was tougher. He cried out and tried desperately but briefly to make a fight of it before he died. And when the fourth man turned and asked softly what the hell the matter was, he used his last breath.

Rocklin slipped into the tent as silently as he could, but there was a double flap of canvas at the entrance, and there was a slight abrasive sound above the noise of the rain. Inside the tent, too, there was light from a dying fire, and the first thing Rocklin saw was a man leaning over the sleeping figure of Rose Legrande.

At that instant, John Claude Legrande woke

with a start. So did his wife. She started to cry out when she saw the strange face peering at her from just inches away.

Another outlaw, who had heard the whisper of the canvas when Rocklin entered, pressed back into a shadowed corner and waited to see what Rocklin was up to. When Rocklin hurled himself at the man crouching over Mrs. Legrande, his cohort pulled a gun and stepped out of his corner. As Rocklin was using his knife on the crouching figure, Legrande was using his crutch to knock the other outlaw's feet from under him. Rocklin whirled when he heard the commotion, kicked the man's gun away, and struggled with him briefly before killing him.

"Thanks," he told Legrande.

"Any time," Legrande replied.

They both looked at Mrs. Legrande. She was sitting clutching her blankets to her throat and staring at the dead men. She looked at Rocklin, then at her husband, who got to his feet and started toward her. She thought of her daughter and got up and went to the bunk. Priscilla was sitting up in bed, horrified at the scene; she had seen it all. Rose Legrande looked around for Dick, didn't see him and screamed, "Dick!"

Rocklin stepped toward her and said in an urgent whisper, "It's all right. He's all right. He heard them and came to wake me. Do you understand, he's all right. I'll go get him. Don't anyone make any more noise; there may still be someone out there. I'll go see as soon as I get Dick."

Dick paled when he saw the bodies, and took several deep breaths, but he was determined not to let his shock show. Rocklin was picking up one of the dead men and letting him fall around his shoulders. "I'll help," Dick offered.

"Hold the tent flap open, but stay inside," Rocklin said. "We'll need some more fire."

"I'll do it," Legrande said.

When Rocklin had removed the two bodies, he said, "I'll clean up a little here, then I'll be gone awhile, maybe a couple of hours."

"Will anyone else come?" Rose Legrande asked.

"Not tonight."

"We'll be all right," Legrande said. "You have enough guns here to hold off an army, and all of us can shoot."

"How many did you kill?" Dick asked.

Rocklin didn't answer. He went out the back of the tent and brought in some strong soap, dipped a pan of hot water from the tub at the fireplace, and started scrubbing the canvas floor of the tent.

"I want to do something," Priscilla Legrande said.

Her father said, "You may get up if you stay warm and don't get too tired. Wrap your blankets around you."

"But she has to stay down, John," her mother protested, "for at least a week."

"We don't have a week, Rose. She must get as strong as she can as fast as she can." He turned to Rocklin. "What is the situation, Mr. Rocklin?"

Rocklin had to choose his words. He knew they should be leaving at once, but it wasn't possible.

"Priscilla can use some more rest and nourishment," he said. "We'll pull out tomorrow as soon as it is dark and hope the rain slacks off."

"I'll bury the outlaws in the forest, hide their saddles, and turn their horses loose. If their boss has to wonder what happened to them, it will buy us some time. My guess is that he suspects you're here, but he isn't sure. He sent his men to find out, and he won't make another move until he has an idea what happened to them.

"Remember, there's plenty to keep him worried—the weather, the lack of fuel up on the mesa, the soldiers. We'll give ourselves another day, and then I'll take you as far as Granite Pass Road. There are some troopers encamped there. You'll be safely on your way to Pine Hollow."

"If it's me you're worried about," Priscilla said, "I can leave tonight."

"I have things to do tonight," Rocklin said.

"Let me go with you," Dick begged. "I'm strong. I can help."

"No. I don't want you to be spotted," Rocklin told him.

"It's raining too hard," Dick argued. "Besides, if they spot you carrying bodies, what difference will it make?"

"That's enough, Dick," Legrande said.

"It's out of the question," Rose Legrande said. "John. Mr. Rocklin. He's just a boy."

John Claude Legrande turned and looked at his wife. He had always adored the way her straw-colored hair softened her strong, straight, but rather sharp features. How, indeed, her hair

135

softened her whole strong and straight person.

In her culture, little girls learned to sit up straight and stand up straight, a habit of a lifetime. Rose Legrande was still standing straight, but the tension lines in her face showed she was holding herself together with a determined command of will. He wanted to go to her, put his arms around her, assure her that she and her children would soon be safe.

"The situation calls for a man, and he's elected," he told his wife. He turned to Rocklin. "If it's all right with you."

Rocklin had finished cleaning up the blood. He nodded.

"I'll borrow a gun, if it's all right," Dick said. He wanted to be loaded for bear.

Rocklin brought him down to earth. "A shovel will be more useful."

"Mr. Rocklin, I beg of you," Rose Legrande said.

"Let him go, Mother," Priscilla said. "I would do something if I could."

Rose Legrande almost laid down an ultimatum, a promise to her husband that if anything happened to her son, she would never forgive him. But she would be airing intimate family matters in front of a stranger. Training was stronger than her strongest instinct.

Rocklin went to fetch Buck, and when he got back to the tent, Dick was shivering with excitement and almost dancing around with impatience.

In three trips they had the six bodies in the deep woods. Rocklin lit a lantern, and he and Dick set to work. The rain had softened the ground, and it didn't take them long to dig six shallow graves. The dead men's horses were standing drearily in the rain, ground-hitched, just outside Rocklin's boundary, and he led them into the woods, hid their saddles and bridles in deep underbrush, and slapped their haunches. They disappeared into the trees.

Rocklin and Dick stayed among the trees, riding double, on their way to the Army encampment. The man on guard was jumpy. He challenged them and pointed his gun, but he couldn't make them out in the dark.

"Stay out of sight," Rocklin told Dick. He went through the routine of "Halt, who goes there?" to "Advance and be recognized," and then asked for Lieutenant Schroeder.

"He's down at the river," the sentry said. "There's been an accident." The trooper was green. Too green for Rocklin to trust.

"Who's in command here?" Rocklin asked.

"Sergeant Clancey."

"Get him."

Sergeant Clancey was more wary, but Rocklin was a convincing man when he had to be. "Tell Lieutenant Schroeder I have a message from Colonel Race. It's urgent."

"Who are you?" the sergeant wanted to know.

"A messenger from Colonel Race. Now! Sergeant."

Lieutenant Schroeder was hollow-eyed, almost dropping from exhaustion. But he recognized the name Rocklin and said, "Yes sir. What can I do?"

"I need an ambulance or a wagon here tomorrow afternoon. Can you manage it?" Rocklin asked.

"Our ambulance is at Rand," Schroeder said, "but a wagon is on the way now. Part of the slide gave way, and my men were downriver from it. Two of them are dead and one is badly injured."

"Bad luck," Rocklin said, "Could you have it back here in the afternoon? It won't seem strange, having it standing by, in the circumstances."

"It will be here," Schroeder promised.

"Are more men coming up here?" Rocklin asked.

"A few at a time. We're stretched very thin, though."

"Have as many men as you can spare take up posts at the waterfall. Take anybody they see coming out from behind the fall into custody."

"From behind the fall?"

"Yes. Weren't you briefed?"

"Of course. The waterfall, yes." The man was out on his feet.

"Warn your men that anyone coming out of there will shoot to kill. Is that clear?"

"It's clear."

"Then I'll see you just after dark tomorrow."

"Yes sir."

"Oh. Do you have any civilians in uniform who have been told to report to you?"

"Yes I have. Four of them."

"Send them up to the fall. They'll know what they're up against."

"Yes sir."

When Rocklin and Dick returned to camp the

rain had slacked off and there was faint light in the east. They stopped outside the tent to gather armloads of firewood, and then pushed through the flaps. Mr. and Mrs. Legrande were at Priscilla's bunk, and Mrs. Legrande had a protective arm about the girl. A big man was sitting on a bench by the fireplace with a shotgun pointed at Rocklin's head.

Dick threw his load of wood at the man, but his aim wasn't very accurate. The man drew back his legs, shifted on the bench, and kept the gun aimed steadily at Rocklin.

"You said no one would come," Rose Legrande blurted at Rocklin.

"Be quiet, Rose," Legrande said. "Come over here, Dick." Dick did as he was told. "I'm sorry, Rocklin." Legrande didn't offer any excuses.

Rocklin took his time stacking his wood behind the fireplace. Then he picked up Dick's and stacked it. Finally, he turned to the man with the shotgun and said, "So you're Big Jim Haggard."

The big man nodded and said, "So you're Rocklin."

Rocklin was irritated, but he wasn't surprised. There were too many people around who had heard his name, people at the fort, probably some of the agents drifting into Pine Hollow and Rand, even a couple of people at the Cattlemen's Association in Chicago.

"I'm sorry to do it this way, but I have to talk to you," Haggard said.

Eighteen

"I made a bad mistake at the beginning," Big Jim Haggard said. "And you're the only chance I have left to make it right."

He and Rocklin were sitting on flat rocks at Rocklin's camp in the corral. There was a small fire and a big pot of coffee.

"All I did at first was give them safe access to the mesa through Rand. They were already up there. One of the men in the gang knew the waterfall trail from long ago. But Heller knew it wasn't safe, and he knew there was a way down through Rand. Hell, he could see it from the top. So I let him use it, if he would leave my cattle and my gold shipments alone."

"This is not going to do any good, Haggard," Rocklin warned.

"Wait. You've got to listen. Later . . . Well, I won't whine about it. Like a fool, I gambled in the beef market, instead of sticking to my ranch where

141

I belong." Haggard was having a hard time getting it out. He was almost choking on it. "I took money from him," he blurted. "A loan, I thought, and . . . Well, the upshot is that I've been his unwilling partner ever since."

Rocklin was unimpressed.

"Dammit, he had me where the hair's short! Can't you see!"

"You knew him before," Rocklin said.

Haggard hesitated, then said, "Since we were boys in the Panhandle. There wasn't anyone my age in a hundred miles until his family came in from Arkansas. Sure, we were wild kids, but that's all. When he . . . Well, never mind. We parted company, that's all." He stood up. He was a handsome man. As tall as Dain Heller, except he was partly bald, and his girth indicated that he had spent more time at a desk lately than in a saddle.

"I want to help, Rocklin. I've got to know that he's dead."

Rocklin was shaking his head.

"He'll get away, don't think he won't. He's dumb. He's almost a halfwit. But he knows what you're thinking. It's uncanny. I don't know how he knows, but he knows."

"You've talked to him?"

"Not for more than a year. He knows I'm out to get him, if I can. He'll kill me the first chance he gets. I state that as a fact. He won't care how he does it, see? This is my only out, Rocklin."

"No. I can't take the risk."

"I have fifty men. It'll probably take twice that many to *make sure* he doesn't get out."

"I can't trust your men."

Haggard turned red. "They're the best men around," he said in a different voice. It wasn't the voice of a woolly lamb.

"That's not what I mean, and you know it. There's always a weak link. It doesn't even have to be a traitor, just some cowpoke who likes to talk. Doesn't Heller know every move you make?" Haggard's face was sufficient answer. "What about Slate?"

"What about him?"

"He's with Heller."

"Impossible. I don't believe it!"

"You see? Sorry, no. I can't trust you. Even if I believe you, I can't trust you. You must see that."

"I can . . ."

"No. You've always known they could be trapped up there. Why didn't you do it?"

"You don't understand, Rocklin . . ."

"Stop using that name. I'm going to have to kill you, Haggard."

"Listen! He would know what I was going to do before I did it. If I could have been *sure* he couldn't get away . . ."

"Where does the north trail come out?" Rocklin asked.

"Back of the saloon," Haggard said, and sat down.

Rocklin eyed him for a minute. "You've seen

143

the Legrandes."

"You've got to get them out of here, Rocklin. Today. Now!"

"The girl's not able to travel yet."

"She has to travel. They'll hit you, Rocklin. When you least expect it. He knows what you're thinking. Get them out. Now."

"Into a trap that you helped set?"

Haggard flushed again. He stood up, his hand on his gun. But he knew about Rocklin, and he just stared at him until he regained control. "You don't believe that," he said.

"Yes, I do. I can't afford not to believe it. Use your head, Haggard. You claim you didn't even know about Big Nose Slate."

The big rancher turned and started toward the crosscut.

"What about your placer operation?" Rocklin asked. "Is it running out of color?"

The question stopped Haggard. He turned and stared at Rocklin. "You've earned your reputation, haven't you? No, it isn't. But I'm claiming it is. Heller's been taking half of everything. I'm gradually closing it down until he's dead. I'm the one who pointed you to the waterfall trail, did you know that?" Haggard asked.

"Yes. What about young Riddle?"

"Who's he?"

Rocklin shook his head. "Don't go through that way. It's too light outside. Go out here and head straight for the trees."

Haggard was looking at the ladder into the

144

airshaft. "I see you discovered my plan to get up on the mesa," he said. "Did you make it?"

Rocklin almost killed him then and there, but he simply didn't want to do it. "Was that your reason for this fake mine?" he asked.

"Yeah. I figured it as close as I could, the airshaft, I mean. I knew the stream was up there. I figured if I could get enough men up there . . . Aw, the hell with it."

"Somebody caught on?"

"I was afraid they had. Do you hear that? I was afraid."

Rocklin shook his head again. "Sorry, Haggard. I can't take the chance. You ought to know that."

"I see your point of view. You want to kill me right now, don't you. Why don't you do it?" The answer was in Rocklin's eyes. Haggard turned and left.

Hank Bowdry came into the big front room where Heller was sitting close to a potbellied stove, shook the rain out of his slicker, and said, "Not a trace."

"Did you check the woods? They're buried there."

"We couldn't read any sign in there, Dain. It's been raining steady. They took off, that's all. It's cold and wet up here, and we're almost out of wood."

"He killed them," Heller insisted with dogged

rage. "Is the quarantine still on at Rand?"

"It is. There is something, though. Shifty says he saw someone who wasn't the miner toss a bucket of water out the front of the tent. But he admits he didn't get a good look at the person, just turned around and saw someone holding a bucket like they'd just emptied it, and going behind the log wall. The reason he's pretty sure it wasn't the miner . . . well, he said it could've been a woman."

"Could have been! Could have been! Was it or wasn't it?"

"It was raining . . ."

"They're there! Get some men together. Ten or twelve. You're going down there to get them."

"One more thing," Bowdry said. "There are four or five troopers camped among the rocks just below the fall. And that's another thing. If it keeps on raining like this, we're not going to be able to get down that way without drowning. You should see that fall."

Heller rose from the chair he was sitting in, and smashed it against the wall. "He's not going to get away with it, damn him to hell! Take a dozen men. Wait 'til it's raining hard. Have six of them walk down first, wait behind the fall until they see a good chance, and sneak up on the pony boys. Don't do any shooting unless you have to.

"When the other men hear a signal, or shooting, they bring the horses and come running. Get those two kids and the woman and bring them back here. Tell the old man, a million dollars. A million dollars and a clear road out of here."

"If we waited for dark—"

"No, no! The first good chance you get! Wait for a good heavy rain and go! *He'll* be waiting for dark, dammit!"

Nineteen

The girl was sitting on the bench near the fire when Rocklin entered the tent. He had been getting Buck and the mule ready to go, and he had packed his bedroll. "How do you feel?" he asked Priscilla.

"Very good," she said. "A little trembly when I stand up, but I'm ready." She didn't look at him when she spoke. Dick had told his family about the other dead men.

"We aren't leaving yet, are we?" Rose Legrande asked. "You said after dark." She was cutting vegetables into a pot of broth. John Legrande and Dick were cleaning guns. They handled them with respect.

"There are heavy rain clouds coming in. If there's a downpour we'll move," Rocklin said.

"But that's absurd," Rose Legrande said. "Do you want her to have a relapse?"

"What is it, Rocklin?" Legrande asked.

"It's time to leave," Rocklin said. "There'll be a

wagon waiting at Granite Pass Road. You should all eat something. Dress in the most protective clothes you can find, and warm plenty of blankets to take along. It won't be a long trip, not much more than a mile, but we have to leave as soon as the rain starts."

"I'm ready," Dick said.

"Lie down until your food is ready," John Legrande told Priscilla. "We're about to start for home."

Rocklin had been watching for the men of Heller's gang who had been picketing the southern boundary of his camp for days. He hadn't seen them for a couple of hours, and he didn't like it. He thought he had heard sounds like gunshots a few moments before, but because of the distant sound of thunder and the constant tattoo of rain, he knew he couldn't be sure.

A vicious crack of lightning blasted the rim of the mesa just above the camp, and the thunder crashed down. The rain came with a roar.

"We're going now," Rocklin said. "I'll go get the mounts and bring them to the front of the tent. Legrande, you'll ride with your daughter on Buck. Dick, look after your mother on the mule."

"What will you do?" Dick asked.

"I'll walk. It's not that far. I'll be right back."

He was maneuvering the mule in close to the log wall when a different kind of lightning struck. He didn't even have time to think that he had failed; he simply went down with a head wound. He hit the ground and rolled for cover in a jumble of rocks before total blackness descended. He didn't hear the roar of guns as a half-dozen men fired through an opaque curtain of rain at the spot where he had been standing.

John Claude Legrande was bundling Priscilla up when the roar came. He said, "Get down," and pushed her to the floor.

Rose Legrande paused in wrapping a blanket around herself and stared at the front of the tent, as if someone was trying to enter her boudoir while she was dressing.

Dick jumped for the gun case, took out two .44 caliber six-guns, yelled, "Here, Dad," and tossed one to him. He cocked his gun and aimed it at the bulge that was moving along between the flaps.

"Wait until you see who it is," Legrande warned him urgently. They soon saw. Two of Heller's men burst through the flap and were shot dead. But others were already at the back of the tent. When they stumbled in, father and son turned and fired. One of the men went down, but that was the end of the battle.

More men were coming swiftly through the front. Legrande went to his knees from a gun chop to the head, and two men overpowered Dick, while trying to fend off two kicking and pummeling women.

"Don't kill him, you fool," Hank Bowdry yelled at the man who had hit Legrande. More men poured through the flap and the women were quickly subdued. "Take the boy and the women."

"She's been ill with pneumonia, you fool!" Rose Legrande screamed.

Legrande was struggling up from the floor.

"She'll be no good to you dead," he told Bowdry.

"We'll take care of her," Bowdry said. "Get them out of here fast," he ordered. "The pony boys will be coming to see what all the fuss is about. Move, move!"

Dick was fighting wildly. "Where's Mr. Rocklin?" he yelled. "What have you done to him?"

"Who?" one of Bowdry's men asked.

"The miner," Legrande said. "The miner."

"He's dead," the outlaw said.

"Move, I said! Get them out of here!" Bowdry shouted.

The Legrandes were hustled out of the tent and dragged onto horses, then the group headed along the cliff toward the falls.

When Sergeant Clancey heard the volley of shots, he didn't know what to do. They didn't seem to be coming from the waterfall, where the four civilian gunmen had taken cover. The sound was faint; it seemed to be coming from farther along the bluff. It made him wonder what had happened to the men at the fall.

He had to make a decision, and make it quickly. He had only ten men at his camp, and two of them had gone to get the wagon the civilian honcho had ordered out of a mudhole. And he couldn't leave the encampment unguarded. Or could he? The camp was in among the trees. Nobody could see it in the rain. Nobody could see anything in the damn rain. Why would anyone be shooting at something he couldn't see?

He left the sentry at the camp, sent four men who had seen the waterfall before and knew roughly where it was, toward the fall, and took three with him toward the sound of the shooting.

After an hour of stumbling around in the dark and the muck, all he and his men found at Rocklin's camp was a nice warm tent and the smell of cooking stew—and a mule standing patiently in the rain. Buck had disappeared while the outlaws were in the tent.

The four troopers who went toward the waterfall found four bodies soaked with rain-diluted blood. They had been off their guard in the downpour, and their throats had been cut.

Bowdry and his men made it back to the falls without encountering anyone. When they stopped, one of the men said, "I thought I saw a light."

"They've probably found the bodies," Bowdry said. "They're only fifty yards from here." He pulled Legrande off his horse and told him, "Walk along the cliff until you hit the road, then turn east. That's left. Have the million dollars back here in three days. If there are any soldiers anywhere within five miles, you're all dead. Get going."

"You know I can't get a million dollars in three days. If you don't talk straight, *everybody* will be dead before this is over. Including you. Do you think they have a million dollars in the Russell Junction bank? Talk straight, if you can."

"You have some leeway. But get it as fast as

you can."

"I can't get it at all without my wife. Every dime I have is held jointly with her. You'd better understand how it is, or there will be a lot of dying for nothing."

"And you'd better understand, mister. If things don't go the way I say, I don't care if I die or not. I don't care who dies. And every man here feels the same way."

"Then I tell you again—talk straight. Pass that on to your boss. I will do what you say, but I can't order the world, anymore than you can. I'll get the money, but not without my wife. It's not possible. But if my girl dies, or if I don't find both of my children alive and well, the million dollars will be the price on your heads. Every two-bit bum and piece of trash in the country will be after you. All of you. That's straight."

"Then this is straight," Bowdry said. "We're up a tree. We don't care who dies. Take your wife and get the money."

Twenty

Rocklin opened his eyes to a murky light and a steady drizzle. He had a four-inch gouge in his scalp behind his left ear, and because of the rain it was still oozing blood. He felt it gingerly. There was a furrow in his skull, probably shallower than it seemed by touch, but close enough to the brain to have put him out for hours.

He heard Buck speak to him softly from nearby. The horse had tried to get to him, but the surrounding boulders blocked it. He got carefully to his feet, leaned on Buck with his arm hooked over the saddle horn to steady himself, and looked around. He wasn't more than ten yards from the entrance to his tent.

The fireplace was cold, and the broth had congealed on top, but he skimmed off the fat and drank some anyway. He had to get away. And right now. Obviously, they had left him for dead, but if he had the measure of Dain Heller, the man would want some proof. All of his weapons were gone from the portable case, but he still had his knife, his .38 in a shoulder holster, and his rifle in Buck's saddle scabbard. There were still some dry clothes in the tent, and he hurriedly changed his shirt and jacket, put his slicker on again and was on his way.

It was slow going. He had to rest occasionally when he became dizzy and started to black out, but the occasions were less frequent as he headed for the fort. He bypassed Pine Hollow, took time to see if anyone had spotted him and picked up his trail, and when he was sure he was in the clear, pushed Buck into a run.

Colonel Race was surprised to see him. "You're supposed to be dead," he said.

"Good. Let's keep it that way. I'd like to use your telegrapher again."

"He's yours. But first you're going to see the surgeon. You don't look too well."

"Later."

"No. Now. Or no telegrapher."

"It's not too deep, but you've definitely lost some skull," the surgeon, a major named Cox, said. "You'll have to rest for a day or two."

"I can't. Not now."

"Be sensible, Rocklin," Colonel Race said. "You'll be no good dead, or disabled."

"Does Heller still have the Legrande children?" Rocklin asked.

"Yes."

"The girl hadn't quite recovered from a bout of pneumonia. Now is not too soon. I can get them back, but it's a one-man job."

"You're going to have a dent in your skull where the hair won't grow," the surgeon said, "unless you want me to cut a little to loosen the scalp around the wound, then pull the skin together and suture it."

"Do it. I don't want to frighten my wife to death when I get home." The colonel and the surgeon glanced at each other in surprise, and Race almost said, "Your wife?" but thought better of it.

"Are you sure you have to do it alone?" Race asked.

"No. But once I get the boy and girl, we can only come down one at a time. I don't want anyone trapped at the top of the escape route. It would be like shooting fish for those killers. They would enjoy it." Rocklin paused, then said, "I had a thought, though."

"Let's hear it," Race said.

"After I get them out of there, why don't we just load the two trails with dynamite and close them tight. Let Heller and his bunch rot up there. It would save a lot of trouble, and maybe lives."

Race was staring thoughtfully at Rocklin. "I don't think the Army would ever sanction it," he said.

"I'll tell you something," Rocklin replied. "About eight years ago, three families in covered wagons heading for Tucson were attacked by the Heller gang. It was in the middle of the desert summer. They were stripped of everything, and their water barrels were shot full of holes. They tried to walk to water, fifteen miles away, and the

157

soles of their feet blistered through their shoes. When they were found—men, women and children—they were dried up like jerky. Every fleshy place on their bodies had shriveled up and died. They had no lips, no earlobes. Their eyelids had shriveled, exposing their eyeballs. Their faces looked like skulls . . ."

"I've seen men staked out by Indians, and baked in the sun," Race said. "So has the major. Even so. Even the Heller bunch. There would be outcries from humanitarians all over the country. Do you mean it?"

"I don't know," Rocklin admitted. "But they're all going to die anyway. Why go through the ritual pretense that we're so civilized?"

"I was ordered to cooperate fully with you," Race said.

Rocklin didn't take the trouble to encode his message to Bannister—the name and address were a blind, anyway.

WILL GO UP AFTER LEGRANDE CHILDREN TONIGHT AT DUSK. HAVE MEN IN FORCE AT WATERFALL AND AROUND SALOON AT FOOT OF BLUFF ONE QUARTER MILE NORTH OF CENTRAL RAND. CONSIDER CLOSING TRAILS WITH DYNAMITE. CONSULT THOSE HIGHEST LEVELS. R.

When the telegrapher had left Race's office, Rocklin said, "I will rest for a few hours, Colonel, if there's a cot somewhere. No point in getting up there before sunset."

"Take your pick," Race said. "The fort's practically deserted."

Rocklin slept like the dead for four hours, and had to be wakened by the colonel's orderly. The pounding headache he had had since he woke up in the rain early that morning had eased off, and he sat on the cot considering his next step. As far as he knew, none of Heller's bunch had ever seen Buck, and now he was glad he had taken that precaution. He washed, shaved his beard off, and went to see the colonel.

"I need some different clothes," he told Race, "and I don't want to spend any time in town. Can you help?"

"You might find something at the sutler's store, if you're not too choosy." He thought a minute and said, "How about a uniform, or at least parts of one?"

"Good. Just the thing," Rocklin said. "I don't need the whole package, and it doesn't have to be new."

"I understand. We can fix you up. What about your bay? Won't it give you away?"

"I've been using a mule."

"Ah. Yes. No one who isn't acquainted with you will know you. However . . ."

"Go on," Rocklin said.

"You could use a haircut," Race told him. "The sutler can handle that for you for a dime."

"I'll do it. Thanks."

When Rocklin rode out of the fort he was a different man. The crazy miner on the mule was no more. Also, he had a new Army Colt .45 besides his own weapons and plenty of ammunition.

"Put 'em as near to the center of town as you can," Dain Heller told Bowdry. "If they come at us from any direction, kill 'em. Post men at both trails down out of here, four men each. That miner's not going to get them out of here alive."

"The miner's dead," Bowdry reminded his boss. "I shot him myself and saw him go down."

"What do you mean, you saw him go down? Didn't you see him after that?"

"We were busy, Dain. It was pouring down rain. You couldn't see much of anything."

"You didn't make *sure?*"

Bowdry, who had ridden with Heller for twenty years, took a step back and put his hand on his gun, without knowing he did it. He thought Heller was going to come at him with his pig-sticker and cut his throat.

"You didn't see his body?"

"No, Dain, I—"

"Go find him. Go find him right now!"

"I can't get down there! They'll have twenty men around that fall."

"We've squeezed through tighter places. Put a dozen men at the rim and lay down a fire. You've got to do it, Hank. I've got to know. Don't you understand that!"

"If the rain keeps up—"

"That's right. Go now before it slacks off. Bring me an ear or something. Do you understand? I've got to know!''

Bowdry made sure there was a fire going at a shack near the center of town, and told some of the men to take the kids there.

They had been asleep all night, huddled behind Heller's potbellied stove. Now they were awake and hungry and scared.

"My father will track you down and kill all of you," Dick told Heller.

"Is the cabin ready?" Heller asked the men sent by Bowdry.

"Yes."

"Get 'em out of here, then." As Dick and Priscilla were being hustled out, he yelled, "Put plenty of men around the place. Don't let anyone near them." He had a thought. "Wait. How many men are posted?"

"Eight."

"Don't put them around the cabin where the kids are. Just leave one man there. Inside. Post the rest at a cabin a couple of doors away. Git!"

There was a roadblock up the hill west of Pine Hollow. It had been set up by Big Nose Slate and three of Heller's men whom he had deputized. When Rocklin pulled up, Slate said, "This is as far as you go."

"Who are you?" Rocklin asked.

Big Nose pulled back his slicker and showed his badge. "I'm the sheriff. This road has been closed. Turn around and go back."

"I'm Stenbrunner from the *Herald,* Sheriff. I've

been authorized in writing by John Claude Legrande to group and cover this story until he and his wife get here. And even after that."

Big Nose was staring at Rocklin, his eyes narrowed. "I don't know you," he said.

"How could you? I can get the Army to escort me up, don't think I can't," Rocklin said. "Shall I do that?"

Big Nose kept staring at him. Rocklin knew he was in trouble.

"Let's see the writing," the sheriff said.

The light was going. Time was running out. Rocklin reached inside the old Army officer's tunic that the colonel had given him, pulled out his .38 and killed the sheriff. Three men were trying to steady their horses and get guns from under their oilskins. Rocklin shot two of them before they cleared leather, but the third was faster. His gun was up and pointed when a rifle slug severed his spine. Rocklin's .38 lead hit him a split second later.

When the smoke cleared, Rocklin looked up the road and saw young Riddle standing at the edge of the forest, rifle in hand. Rocklin rode toward him and said, "That was good timing. Thanks."

"I knew you weren't dead," Riddle said. "I've been watching for you."

Rocklin was fully alert, and his gun was still in his hand. "How did you know?" he asked.

"Are you thinking of shooting me again?" Riddle asked, grinning. "I just knew, that's all."

"How many men from your outfit have gone up this trail?"

"Twelve men from the railroad, and about twenty other men. How did you get them here so fast?"

"Come with me," Rocklin ordered. Riddle didn't hesitate. He fetched his horse from among the trees, holstered his rifle, and mounted.

Bowdry looked like a drowned rat. Blood was dripping down his wet hand and off the ends of his fingers. "I lost three more men, Dain. And what for? How many is that now? Twelve? Fifteen?"

"Did you find the body?"

"How could I? The pony boys have—" He had started to say that the troopers had already picked up the body, but he didn't finish. Dain Heller pulled a gun and shot him.

"Get out!" he yelled at the other mud-soaked men, who were standing there staring down at Bowdry, unbelieving.

Twenty-One

Rocklin and Riddle scouted the camp at the mine for an hour before closing in from both sides. The place was dead. Trashy and woebegone in the ceaseless rain. Inside the tent, Riddle lit a match and looked around.

"A good idea," he said. "What made you think of it?"

"The mine seemed promising when I read about it in a report by a competent man. It was a way of making them come to me. Too many men had been killed trying it the other way. I sort of hope the man who wrote the report isn't dead, too. I relied on it a lot."

"You're Rockland, aren't you?" Riddle said.

"Where did you get that?"

"Picked it up in gossip. You know how agents are when they get together. Worse than old women. I didn't believe there was such a man."

"I'm dead now. Don't forget that. And it's Rocklin. So much for gossip. No more, do you hear?"

"Yes, sir. I'm glad you liked my report."

"You wrote that?"

"Yes sir."

"Fine job. The map was invaluable. You can help me some more by never telling anyone that I'm alive."

"I won't. Sir, why did you bring me along? You've never done that before, have you?"

"I'm having a dizzy spell now and then. If I black out, it's up to you. Come on." Rocklin lit a lantern, and they made their way through the crosscut toward the fake airshaft. "They must know you're an agent by now," Rocklin said. "Why haven't they killed you?"

"They figured I was so dumb, it would be more interesting to watch and see what I was up to."

Rocklin smiled in the dark. "Good dodge. I'll remember it."

"It wouldn't work with you, sir. You look too . . . too much in charge, I guess."

When they reached the airshaft, Rocklin said, "I'll go first." He started up the ladder carrying the lantern.

"I'll be jiggered," Riddle breathed. "Perfect."

"There it is," Rocklin said, after they had crawled out of the hole and made their way up to the cluster of juniper. They could see three feeble lights through the miserable rain.

"What's your plan?"

"I'm not sure yet," Rocklin said. "First, I have to scout the place and see if I can spot where the girl and boy are being held. I'll pick up an armful of brush and twigs, and just walk in. Nobody will pay any attention to me. It's not exactly a neighborly town. It might take awhile, though. Give me two hours. Let's get back down, I want to show you something in case I don't get back."

When they had scooted back down the hill a way, Rocklin said, "Remember your drawing of the mesa. It was remarkably good, and it was to scale. We're only about a half mile from the waterfall, and only ten or twelve yards in from the edge of the mesa. The town is about a mile southwest of here. Here, look. Light a match. Here's my compass. If it's raining so hard you can't see, take a heading of two hundred and twenty-five degrees. All right?"

"I gotcha."

"You probably won't have any trouble going in, because of the lights. But it will be different coming back. Especially if it's raining hard. Of course, you come back at forty-five degrees."

"Of course."

"It's up to you, though. You're the one who'll be on the spot. You might decide to go straight on out to the waterfall. If so, head a hundred and thirty-five degrees from the center of town. You'll get there. Heller will probably have more than one guard at the top of the waterfall trail, though. I'm on my way."

"Good luck, Rocklin."

It occurred to Rocklin that it had been a long time since he had had someone along on a job who said good luck.

"You too," he said, and left.

The rain eased off to a sprinkle as Rocklin

approached Rathole with his armful of juniper branches and chunks of old wood. He saw no one at all until he neared the cabin with four men at the back door and four at the front. He walked by it two cabins away, next to a shack with a dim light inside, and blankets or something equally heavy over the windows. A couple of guards glanced his way as he slushed toward the center of the strange town.

He dropped his wood at a shack that looked deserted, and slipped back toward the guarded cabin. He picked a spot in a shadowed corner formed by a woodshed that was attached to a house, and settled back on his heels to wait.

He could hear indistinct voices that sounded vaguely disgruntled, catching only a word now and then. It sounded as if Hank Bowdry had been killed. If that was true—and Rocklin hoped it wasn't—there would be nobody to restrain Heller. He distinctly heard the word "crazy."

An hour passed. He had to move cautiously to relieve a leg cramp, and one of the guards glanced his way. He felt light-headed, and all he could do was take several slow, deep breaths. Another painfully slow half hour passed. He would have to leave pretty soon or Riddle would be coming.

One of the men was complaining. "I don't see why we can't build a fire," he said.

"And call attention to this filthy dump?" another man objected.

"Isn't that the idea?"

"Shut up!" someone else said. "I'm tired of listening to you."

So Dick and Priscilla weren't there. Rocklin had to look some more, and he would not get back to Riddle in time. He stood up slowly, and was about to slip around the corner of the shack, when someone walked by not ten feet from him. He smelled cooked salt pork. The man was carrying food.

"Hey, Shorty, when do we eat?" a guard at the cabin called.

"You can starve as far as I'm concerned," Shorty replied. "You're too fat, anyway." When he reached the shack with the dim light, and the blankets for curtains, he said, "Open up, Ned." A few seconds later, the door creaked inward, and Shorty slipped inside.

Rocklin was going to miss Riddle if he didn't hurry, but he could not rush now. The rain had eased off to a sprinkle, and he could not be seen sneaking around town at this point.

He paused at the edge of town and looked around. He was alone. He looked at his watch, holding it up to his eyes. He was twenty minutes overdue. Riddle was on his way. Maybe almost in town, unless he had decided to give Rocklin a little more time.

Rocklin stayed put. He knew it would be too easy to miss stealthy movement in the dark. Ten minutes passed. Fifteen. A shadow moved faintly out on the mesa. It moved again. It was coming right toward him. It started pouring rain again. Rocklin hurried to intercept Riddle and said, "Let's get out of here."

"It's not going to be easy," Riddle said, after

169

Rocklin described the setup.

"I think we can do it, but I'll need a diversion. I'll wait here for a half hour while you make your way toward the waterfall trail. Steer five degrees west of south, stay clear of the edge, and you'll have plenty of rocky cover. Do you have a knife?"

"Two knives."

"Good. The sentries won't be expecting anyone from the direction of the town, so you might be able to take care of them quietly, one by one. If you have to shoot, that's all right. The point is to make as much racket as you can, once you start shooting. It'll probably be better for you if they're dead when that happens. How you handle it is up to you, but I'll need enough turmoil to make the gang think that troops are breaking through at the top of the trail, or trying to.

"I'll work my way far enough into the town so I can come at them from the direction of Heller's place, and tell them the troops are coming up, and Heller wants them at the trail. If it's still raining, they won't get a very good look at me.

"I'll probably start toward the fall with them, but I'll ditch them as soon as I can, and head back to the place where the boy and girl are. I know the guard's name. Ned. All I have to do is hope he hasn't been relieved, or something. I'll go in telling him that Heller says to kill the kids. I think I can get them out of there.

"It will take me about an hour to get into position, and about thirty or forty minutes after that to get back to the airshaft.

"Again, it's up to you. You can try to make it to

the shaft, or you can head down the waterfall trail, and take the chance of being shot before you can identify yourself. All right?"

"Right. Good luck."

"One more thing . . . Never mind." It wasn't like Rocklin at all, and Riddle sensed it.

"What is it?"

Rocklin decided he had to speak. "I had a little dizzy spell in town. If I feel myself going again, I'll let you know by setting off a stick of dynamite . . . No, that won't work."

"Dynamite?"

"I brought a stick with me, but . . ."

"Should we try it the other way?" Riddle asked.

Rocklin thought about how hard it would be for Riddle to find the little prison shack in the dark, especially since he had never been in the town. He thought about Dick and Priscilla Legrande. He thought about failure, something he had never done on any kind of job since he was a cabin boy.

"I should have let you scout the town," he said. He had never second-guessed himself, either.

Riddle thought it over before he spoke, then said, "Sir, it's going to take both of us, no matter who goes where."

Rocklin actually put his hand on the young man's shoulder. "I'm on my way," he said.

About an hour after Rocklin rode out of Fort Hatcher, Colonel Race was sitting in his office thinking. Suddenly, he yelled for his orderly, told him to saddle their horses and get ready to go on a little trip. A half hour later they were heading across the flatland to connect with the stage road on their way to Russell Junction, and from there to Rand.

It was late in the evening when they reached their destination and located Lieutenant Gunning. "Who's the engineer in charge of the river project?" Race asked him.

"Major Priestly," Gunning said. He looked as if he hadn't had his clothes off for a week.

"Give him my regards and ask him if he has time to talk to me." Race outranked the major, but the engineers were a law unto themselves when they were on an emergency job. "And then get some sleep," Race told the lieutenant.

"My men haven't slept," Gunning said. He turned and started to leave.

"Wait. How many civilian agents have turned up?"

"I don't know for sure. Twenty or thirty."

"Ask them to report to me, fully armed, at the saloon. Tell the major that's where I'll be."

"Yes sir." Gunning was on his way.

Race went to the saloon, walked in, and ordered a drink. His orderly stepped just inside the door, put his back to the front wall, and stood watching. The bartender promptly set out a full bottle of rye whiskey.

The colonel looked around. Two troopers were sitting with their heads on a table, asleep. There were ten other men at tables in the bar, mine guards. They looked dry and warm.

Race had finished his second drink when the

agents, wearing uniforms, started pushing into the small saloon. When eight of them had come, Race motioned toward the guards and said, "These men are all under arrest. Take their guns. Shoot anybody whose hands move anywhere but up."

The ensuing burst of gunfire was ear-splitting in the small room. When it was over, three outlaws and one agent were dead. The rest of the outlaws were touching the ceiling.

"Get them out of here," Race ordered.

Major Priestly entered just as the last of the hardcases was being pushed out. "It's about time," he said. "Major Priestly," he told the colonel.

"Colonel Race. Thanks for coming, Major. Drink?"

"Later, if you don't mind."

"I want to show you something and get your advice." Race turned to the agents who were still crowding the cramped space. "Some of you men come with me."

He led them through the storage room of the saloon and out the back door, circled the outhouse, and headed for a clump of underbrush at the bottom of the cliff. "Help me clear this away," he ordered.

It was quickly done, and the foot of the north trail to Rathole was right there.

"The major and I are going up a ways," he told the agents. "We may draw some fire from above. If we do, give us plenty of covering fire."

But there was silence from above. Actually, the top of the trail was a quarter of a mile along the rim of the cliff just above the main part of town.

"What I want you to do for me, Major, is tell me just where you would place dynamite, and how much, to close this escape route so tight that a rattlesnake couldn't get through," Race said.

Rocklin missed the center of Rathole by a hundred yards in the rain, and it cost him precious time to get his bearings. When he did, he realized he was on the eastern edge heading for Heller's place.

There were men on horseback circling the town, now—three or four of them, Rocklin guessed. One of them passed within four feet of him. It gave him an idea, and he hoped Riddle's diversion didn't start before another rider passed his way.

The timing couldn't have been better. Another rider, or the same one, was passing almost as close when the sound of shooting came from the direction of the fall. The rider, startled, stopped and turned his horse that way. Rocklin had him off his horse, and his knife in his jugular, in five seconds.

He was riding fast past the big house when Heller jerked the door open. Rocklin could see him only faintly against the flickering light from inside, but it was Heller, all right.

"They're trying to come up the waterfall," he shouted.

"Turn everybody out," Heller shouted back. "Tell those men guarding the house to get up here. Tell Ned to kill the kids!"

Rocklin didn't tarry. He skidded his mount to a stop in front of the guards, kicking up mud everywhere. "They're coming up the trail! Heller says to get up there. Right now!" The men moved.

He pounded on the door of the shack where Dick and Priscilla were, and yelled Ned's name.

"Who is it?" Ned shouted from inside.

"Let me in! Troopers are coming up the trail. Heller says to kill the kids."

The door creaked open, and Ned started to say, "Who are you?" but didn't get it out. Rocklin shot him three times on his way through the door.

Priscilla was huddled on a bunk in the corner, and Dick was aiming a chair at Rocklin's head. He dropped it when Rocklin said, "Hurry up! Come on, come on! It's time to go."

"Mr. Rocklin!" Dick cried. "I knew they couldn't kill you!" He headed toward the door.

"Take a coat," Rocklin said. Priscilla was climbing out of the bunk. Rocklin wrapped blankets around her and carried her out to the horse. She seemed strong enough. She had her arms so tight around his neck, he could hardly breathe.

Two men rode up. "The boss said to kill them," one of them yelled. They were both going for guns, but so was Rocklin, and he was faster.

He tossed Dick aboard one of the dead men's horses, and lifted Priscilla onto the one he had been riding.

"Hey! What's going on?" Two more riders had appeared through the rain. Rocklin threw shots their way, hitting one of them, and shouted, "Let's

175

go! Stay close!" to Dick, and they were on their way.

Men were after them, but Rocklin knew where he was going, and the outlaws didn't. He missed the path down to the old dump by not more than twenty yards. He piled off his mount with Priscilla in his arms, and Dick jumped down. Rocklin slapped the horses on the flank and sent them on their way.

The rain stopped with untimely suddenness, and one of the outlaws yelled, "There they are." Rocklin shot him. He pushed Priscilla and Dick down behind some rocks and lit a stick of dynamite that he had tucked in at his waist, and tossed it up among the juniper bushes. He would send the hunters to cover, and they would think twice before rushing into the open again.

A faint flash to the north caught Rocklin's eye. It was followed by a faint but unmistakable boom, the kind that Rocklin knew could only be made by dynamite. Timing again. He had no guess as to what it might be, and he didn't have time to guess anyway.

He picked up Priscilla and headed for the airshaft. Dick followed closely along, asking questions that Rocklin didn't have to time to listen to.

"You go down first," he told Dick. "It comes out down at the corral."

"Wow!" Dick said. He was having the time of his life, and would be the most popular boy at his prep school for weeks to come.

"You go next, Priscilla," Rocklin said. "You'll have to make it alone."

"I can do it," she assured him. She seemed alert, and as far as Rocklin could tell, she had no fever.

Someone shouted, "What's that? Hey, there he is!"

Rocklin threw some more shots in the direction of the voice, and climbed into the hole after Priscilla. On his way down he did two things: He emptied the Army Colt at the top of the hole, and he lit a fuse. The fuse was attached to a bundle of dynamite that he had placed days before, just as a precaution.

"Hurry!" he urged the young people. "Through the tunnel, Dick. But don't make too much of a racket, and don't rush into the tent. If someone's in there, he might shoot first and look later. Go!"

There was no one in the tent or around it.

"Down," Rocklin said. "On the floor. Quickly!" They did as they were told, and Rocklin lay down between them, holding them close.

The blast was like a sharp earthquake.

"Gee whillikers!" Dick said as Rocklin picked him and Priscilla up, and started brushing the dust off.

It hit him right then. The blast at the other end of the mesa. Race had closed the back door! No doubt about it. Rocklin was astonished and elated. For the first time since he took the job, he felt good about it.

He went to the front of the tent and whistled for Buck, and soon his horse came out of the trees and beat it for the camp. The mule, which Rocklin had turned loose before climbing up to Rathole, was gone for good.

One of Heller's men stepped into the room where his boss was sitting, walked toward him, and pulled a gun from under his slicker.

"What do you think you're doing?" Heller demanded.

"I have bad news," the man said. "I don't want to get shot down like your friend Bowdry."

Heller wasn't very interested in the man's insult or in his news. "Say it and get out."

"The kids got away. Someone helped them."

"That damn miner!" Heller shouted, then he let out an ear-splitting string of curses. "Where's Ned?"

"Dead. Charlie and Spike, too."

Heller cursed some more. "Get the men," he ordered. "We're breaking out of here, now. Git!"

"They're coming up the trail!" the man protested.

"No, they're not. Can you hear any more shooting? It was a trick to draw you jackasses away so the miner could get the kids. Anyway, we're going the other way. Git, I said!"

"Some of the men are still after the kids," the outlaw said.

"They won't get them!"

Just then they heard the sharp dynamite blast, not far from town, and the distant boom immediately afterward.

"What was that?" Heller's man said.

"It's dynamite, you fool. That miner set it off. Where was it? Where did it come from?"

They hurried out to the front porch. It had stopped raining. Riders were milling around, wondering what to do next.

"Where did that come from?" Heller yelled.

"It sounded like over by the old dump," one of his men said.

From the direction of the mine. The picture was instantly clear to Heller. That's what that damn miner had been doing. There was a way up over there. There was more wild cursing, then he shouted, "Go get him! He's crawling into his hole over there! Go get him!"

He was pacing the porch in his rambling, loose-jointed way, waiting for word, when there was a shattering roar from the direction his men had ridden and the ground shook under his house. The miner had plugged the hole. He knew it.

It was too late for cursing. He went inside and stood staring down at his potbellied stove. So now there was only one way out for his men. There weren't so many now. Three more had died at the airshaft when the mesa rumbled with the sound of the blast.

He didn't think about that; he thought about the Rand escape route. He had known instinctively, hearing that distant boom, that the Rand trail had been closed. Well, there was more than one way to skin a cat.

Twenty-Two

Riddle's main problem was getting the sentries at the top of the falls to come out of their holes. They were hunched down among rocks over which they had stretched a canvas shelter, and they weren't about to move for anything less than a major attack. Riddle was almost on top of them before he heard their voices and knew where they were.

There were three of them. Riddle tossed a rock at the sound of rain on canvas and heard one of them say, "What the hell?"

"Well, go see what it was," another said.

"I don't care what it was. I'm staying dry. It's the first time I've been half dry for a week."

"I'll go," the third man said. He was feeling his way along, peering through the rain, when Riddle said softly, "Hey!" and dodged to one side. The man turned swiftly, off balance, and Riddle struck. They were too close to the edge of the cliff, and the

181

man took Riddle's knife with him when he went over. He almost took Riddle.

"What is it?" one of the men called.

"A dead guy," Riddle said hoarsely, getting out his other knife.

"What?" The outlaw crawled from under the shelter.

Riddle didn't wait. He struck again. But the other sentry was right behind his buddy, and he wasn't so easy. Riddle felt a swiping blow down his left side and heard his slicker rip. He went swiftly into a crouch and swung his knife blindly behind him, backhanded. It found a target, and as he rolled away and jerked the knife back, he heard a sound like a grunt.

He lay still for a minute and crept toward the sound. The sentry was lying in the rain bleeding to death, but he gave it one more try as he felt Riddle's presence right above him. His blade ripped Riddle's oilskin from side to side but didn't touch his flesh. Riddle stabbed again and again. It was a strange death struggle between two men down in the mud who couldn't see each other.

When it was over, Riddle started firing wildly into the air, first with a six-shooter, then with a rifle, then with the six-shooter again. He reloaded swiftly in the dark and kept firing. He fired until he was almost out of ammunition, then located one of the horses that had been snorting and whinnying, and headed down the waterfall trail. He could feel the warm blood running down into his boots.

Heller's men, all mounted, were gathered at the front of the big house when Heller stepped out onto the porch. The men were edgy, impatient, and the horses were skittery and noisy. Heller shouted over the snorting of the horses, the nervous talk, and the squeak of leather.

"Settle down," he said. "What's the matter with you?"

"What are we waiting for?" a rider shouted back.

"Shut up!" The men quieted down. "We're going through Rand. Who came in from watch this morning?"

"I did," one of the outlaws said.

"Colter?"

"Yeah."

"What does it look like at that end?" Heller asked.

"There are soldiers around, but most of them are busy at the river. The saloon is still ours, but we have to go easy. We shouldn't go out more than one at a time. We can make it if we go easy."

"Any sign they know about the trail?"

"Nary one."

"Well, they got the kids back," Heller said. "And there ain't any use trying to get down the waterfall trail. Go ahead and git. This'll blow over. We'll meet up here again next spring. Got it?" There was no reply from anyone. "Got it!"

There was some mumbling and a few muttered "yeahs."

Heller knew they would never be back if they had any say about it. If he had had anyone at his side at that moment, he would have thrown down on them.

"What about women and kids?" someone asked. "I ain't leaving mine."

"Take 'em, take 'em," Heller said. "Git going."

"Ain't you coming?" someone wanted to know.

"I'll be along," Heller said. "Ain't you ever heard that a captain is the last man to leave his ship?" He laughed. His men stared at him. Then one of them turned his horse and started away at a run. The rest followed.

Riddle waited for as long as he dared behind the wildly rushing water, then slapped the horse, driving it out into the open. It drew some shots from a cluster of nearby rocks, and he slipped out and took cover behind other rocks. So far, so good.

He heard the dynamite blast up on the mesa and wondered if Rocklin hadn't made it. He didn't hear the distant boom from Rand; the fall was making too loud a roar.

The rain stopped. Riddle had to go back to the camp, climb up the airshaft, and see how Rocklin was doing. He yelled, "Hey! Out there. Hold your fire. I'm coming out."

"Come ahead," someone shouted. It didn't sound encouraging. Four men with their throats cut hadn't put anyone in the mood to take prisoners.

"Hold your fire! My name is Riddle. I'm an agent for the railroad. Is there anyone out there who knows the name? Riddle."

There was silence for a few moments, then someone shouted, more encouragingly, "Come out with your hands up."

Riddle went out. A man came from behind the rocks to meet him. "Riddle?" he inquired.

"Is that you, Smutz?"

"Hell, man, how did you get up there?"

"I need to be patched up. I have to go over to the mine. The Legrande kids should be coming down that way. I'm running out of time."

"Down through the mine? You're crazy!"

"Dammit, do any of you have any bandages? I don't have time to draw you a picture."

"There's a doctor back at camp," Smutz said. "Come on, let me give you a hand."

"I can't sew you up in this light," the doctor said. "I'll wrap you tight enough to stop the bleeding, but you'd better stop running around. Four of your ribs are exposed."

There was a loud boom from the direction of the mine. It seemed to shake the mesa. "He made it down!" Riddle said. "Hurry, hurry!"

He and his men met Rocklin coming along the edge of the forest toward the encampment.

"They're safe! The kids are safe!" Riddle

shouted. But it came out as a hoarse whisper. He looked pale as death in the darkness.

The rattle of gunfire came from the direction of the waterfall.

"They're trying to break out," Riddle said. "Let's go."

"You're not going anywhere, except to the fort," Rocklin said. "They're just letting us know they're there. It's a stalemate for now. They can't get down and we can't get up."

"What do we do, just wait for them to give up?" Riddle asked.

"That would be a good thing for them, and for us. But I don't think they're going to. They'll try the back door first. Then they'll be back. This is the only way out now."

"How do you know?"

"I heard the blast that slammed it shut."

"How do you know that's what it was?" Smutz asked.

"I know. Who's in charge here?"

The agents looked around at each other. One of them said, "You are, I guess."

"Do any of you know Riddle?"

"I do," Smutz said. "Smutz is the name."

"All right, Smutz. Did Colonel Race send up a wagon?"

"Yes. It's here."

"Take a half-dozen men and get the two young people to the fort," Rocklin said. "It's ten miles—"

"I know where it is."

"Don't let them out of your sight. Take Riddle

with you. Don't let him move under his own power until you get him into the post hospital. Pour some hot soup or coffee down him. Is there such a thing at the camp?"

"Yes."

"Good. You're on your way." Rocklin turned to the other men. "Is there a good rider with a fast horse?"

Another man stepped forward. "I'll go."

"What's your name?"

"Axelrod." It was a code connecting the man with Bannister.

"Well, Axelrod," Rocklin said, answering the code, "ride toward Russell Junction. Find the Legrandes there, or intercept them if they're on their way. Tell them their children are safe."

"Right." Axelrod was on his way.

"The rest of you round up every man who can shoot straight and don't let anyone come out of the falls alive, unless they come out with their hands up. My guess is that they'll hit in force a couple of hours from now, as soon as they find out it's this or nothing.

"Has anyone seen Lieutenant Schroeder or Sergeant Clancey?"

"Clancey was at the camp when we left," one of the men said.

When Rocklin found Clancey, he told him, "In about two hours, I'll need every man you can spare, Sergeant. In the meantime—"

"What? Who are you? I don't know you."

"The crazy miner. Come on, Clancey, I shaved.

187

In the meantime . . ."

Clancey held a lantern to Rocklin's face. "I'll be damned," he said. "But you're dead."

". . . why don't you build a couple of fires along your flanks, at the road, and a hundred yards or so north along the cliff."

"I've been told to follow your orders," Clancey said. "But why?"

"They're going to try to break out of there, and we'll be able to see them better. Also, some of your men can get warm and dry for a change. Tell them to stay behind the fires, though. I don't want the gang to get any accurate idea of what they're up against until the time comes. How are things down at the river?"

"Under control. I lost some men."

"I heard. I'm sorry. You might lose some more. This is their only way out now, and I don't think many of them are going to give up. I have a camp at the mine. There's a tent and a fireplace and food. You can use it."

"I've seen it. Thanks," Clancey said. "I have a couple of men in pretty bad shape."

"The wagon the colonel sent is headed for the fort right now," Rocklin said. "Do you have anyone who needs to ride along?"

"No, they'll be all right. But they'll appreciate shelter, and a fireplace."

"Is Pine Hollow still there? Have you heard?"

"Only the north half, this side of the river. The other side's just a big lake. If you ask me, it's an improvement. I'll get my men moved."

*   *   *

Dain Heller sat brooding in front of the stove. He didn't have long to wait. In less than an hour he heard the sound of horses returning from the direction of Rand. He thought his men had probably run into the Rand sentries halfway to the rim, and the sentries had told them the trail wasn't there any longer.

That was in fact what had happened. The sentries were dazed and not very coherent, but managed to make themselves understood under persistent and urgent questioning.

Heller got up and went to the porch to face his men. They were yelling at Heller and at each other. Heller stared at them until they quieted down.

"So the miner thinks he has us treed," he said. "Well, he's got another think coming. We'll go down the waterfall so fast they won't have time to reload."

"We won't make it," one of the outlaws said.

"We have to make it," Heller shouted. "Do you want to stay up here and starve? Or freeze when the real cold weather comes? They can camp down there from now on! We're leaving!"

"You knew this could happen," another voice complained. "Why didn't we pull out a long time ago?"

"Because you weak sisters couldn't get rid of one lousy miner, that's why!"

"You had a chance to kill him, why didn't *you?*"

a new voice chimed in.

Heller didn't answer. "Stay here, then," he said. "They'll have a whole battalion down there by this time tomorrow. I'm leaving."

The outlaws didn't press their useless point any further. Some of them started in a run for the waterfall, and others gradually followed.

Heller mounted and rode after his men for a while, then pulled up gradually and let them go. When they had disappeared in the darkness, he turned back and went into his house. He took an axe and chopped away at the wall behind the big stove. When he had made a big enough hole, he took out a large, beat-up suitcase, laid it on the floor, squatted down, and opened it. It was full of gold certificates.

A voice behind him said, "We kinda thought you might pull something like this." Two of his men had guns pointed at him.

Heller pivoted swiftly on the balls of his feet as he reached under his oilskin. He didn't bring the gun out, he merely pulled the trigger twice. He got up and walked over to the men, now lying on the floor.

"Just like you, Brownie," he said. "Always did shoot off your mouth when you should have been shooting your gun." He kicked the dying man in the face.

He stacked everything in the room in a pile, fetched two cans of kerosene, and splashed the stuff around. Then he picked up the suitcase, paused at the doorway to toss a match, and left in a hurry.

The clouds were moving off to the southeast and the sky above was clear. In the distance, muffled by the wall of the mesa, was persistent gunfire.

And Heller was going from house to house with kerosene and matches trying to burn the water-soaked town of Rathole.

Twenty-Three

Men who needed medical attention and rest had taken over Rocklin's tent, and he was in his bedroll near the fire at the camp. His sleep had been deep for a while; now it was restless, disturbed by a meaningless dream and the sound of gunfire. He woke up with a start. The gunfire was real.

Clancey was leaning over him, about to wake him. Rocklin jumped up, fought off a dizzy spell, and said, "Every man you've got, Clancey."

"They're already up there."

"Can you shoot straight?"

"I certainly can."

"Then come on."

"How many men have come out?" Rocklin asked when he reached the rocks where the troopers and the special agents had taken cover.

"Twelve so far," one of the agents said. "None of them made it."

"I don't think there could have been more than thirty-five men left up there," Rocklin said. "We'll let the rest of them surrender if they want to."

But none of them wanted to. They knew if they didn't get out alive, they'd be dead men anyway, one way or another. They tried a new tactic. Eight or ten of them rushed out on foot and took cover. Then they laid down heavy fire as four mounted men charged out from the fall and made a dash for Granite Pass Road. None of them made it either.

"If they reached the road, they could hightail it over the pass," Rocklin said to Sergeant Clancey.

"It's covered," Clancey replied.

Four more outlaws on horses tried for the road, and died in a storm of lead. Rocklin got off three shots, and all of them hit.

"What are we doing here?" Clancey said. "You don't need any help. I'll bet you're Army, right? Intelligence?"

"Here they come again," Rocklin said. "There can't be many more of them left."

Clancey talked between shots, but it didn't spoil his aim. "You talk like a brigadier, at least."

The gang members behind the rocks who were covering for the riders were being cut down one by one. Troopers and special agents were dead, too, five or six of them. The desperados could shoot.

"Has anyone seen a tall, lanky man come out?" Rocklin asked. "Must be six-foot-five, or maybe six. You couldn't miss him."

"Not me," Clancey said.

"Me either," the agent on the other side of Rocklin said.

"Pass the word," Rocklin ordered. "I need to know."

"What's up?" Clancey asked.

"I'm going in. If we let Heller slip through, we'll have all this to do over again sometime, somewhere."

"By yourself?" Clancey asked. "I take it back. You're too crazy to be Army."

"One man might make it," Rocklin said. "I've been up there. Besides, it's just about all over; no use anybody getting killed who doesn't have to." He motioned for a couple more agents to join him and told them, "I'm going to pull back a little and go along the foot of the mesa, then make my way back along the cliff to the waterfall. Cover me going in, but whatever you do, don't shoot at the fall after I'm behind it. Wait a minute or two. Pass the word. And Clancey . . ."

"Yes sir?"

"Don't follow me in for a while. Wait until it's quiet up there, and then send a scout first."

The stars were out now. The special agents and the soldiers could see Rocklin clearly as he made his way along the base of the cliff, leading Buck.

The outlaws who had come out from behind the fall to give covering fire didn't see Rocklin. They were using up the last of their ammunition in a grim death battle. Rocklin paused in the shadow of the fall and then ran behind it. There was a brief spate of gunfire, and then Rocklin whistled for Buck.

"So far, so good," Clancey said under his breath.

Rocklin squeezed back between the rocks at the

edge of the fall and threw several rifle shots at the men facing the troopers and civilians. There were only four of them left. He didn't shoot to kill, but just to let them know there was someone behind them, and it was time to give up.

It didn't do any good. They stood up and died on their feet, two of them facing the troopers and two facing Rocklin, blasting away.

There were still four men at the top of the waterfall trail, waiting to come down. They had been watching for Heller, but he was busy trying to burn the rest of the town. When he had used all the kerosene he could find, he headed north. The four men didn't wait much longer. It looked as if Heller had plans of his own, and they weren't surprised.

Rocklin surprised them. They could only get down the trail one at a time with their horses, and it wasn't easy to turn a horse around. One of them tried standing on his saddle and jumping over the rocks that bounded the trail. Rocklin let him go, and he disappeared over the cliff. The other three men were jostling each other, and their horses were trying to keep their footing on the mud and rocks of the trail.

Rocklin climbed to a ledge just above the trail and shouted for them to throw down their guns, but they had made up their minds that this was their night to die. Rocklin was in a good position, and the fight was brief.

He avoided the town of Rathole. The old, wet wood gave off an unpleasant, acrid odor as it was burning, and it crackled loudly against the encroaching flames. The light was garish and alive in the crisp clear night.

When the light was behind him, Rocklin thought he got a glimpse of a rider far to the north, but he couldn't be sure. Another dizzy spell hit him, but he pushed Buck into a run and gulped in the clean-smelling air that rushed at him.

Heller wasn't pushing his horse, and he was nearing the Rand escape route when he became aware of a rider behind him. He knew it had to be that damn miner, and he didn't want to tangle with him just now. But he didn't want anyone on his trail, either, no matter who it was. He had planned for this, if the time came when he had to get out in a hurry. He dismounted and unsheathed his long gun.

As soon as Rocklin heard the slug growl past his head, and an instant later the boom, he knew he was up against an old single-shot Sharps rifle with a .45 slug and ninety grains of powder in the cartridge. His fifteen-shot Winchester was a fine gun, but it didn't have the range or, at this distance, the accuracy of the Sharps. He swerved and pulled up behind a clump of juniper.

Heller didn't fire again. He climbed on his horse and headed for the trail. His message was clear to Rocklin: He knew where he was going and he would kill anyone who tried to stop him.

Rocklin had planned to take it slow and easy anyway. After all, the back door had been closed, and Heller wasn't going anywhere. Or was he? He seemed to think he was. Rocklin nudged Buck into a run again, but he stayed clear of the faint trail and took advantage of any cover he could find.

Heller was halfway down the trail when Rocklin spotted him. It was amazing how much a man could see on a clear night at nine thousand feet, especially after so many days of rain as heavy as ink.

The trail stretched straight from the rim of the mesa along an old watercourse to the back of the saloon. Part of it was missing, though, a large section between the town and the saloon a quarter of a mile away. It was plain to see that the side of the mesa had simply been blown away, and where there had once been a trail was now a sheer cliff.

But Heller, who was not blind, was still going. Rocklin headed Buck down the trail, wasting no time. Heller saw him. He pulled out his rifle and took cover. Rocklin found some rocky protection just ahead of another .45 slug. The Sharps was still a very dangerous weapon, but Rocklin was closer now, and the Winchester was a repeater. Rocklin could get off three or four shots while Heller was hand-feeding another cartridge into the Sharps's breech. He made the best of his advantage, but when the Sharps came up, he ducked. And even so, the slug blasted away bits of rock that bit into the side of his face like buckshot.

The strange duel lasted until Rocklin had to reload, and Heller, who had counted Rocklin's shots, took the opportunity to fire three shots into the face of the cliff behind Rocklin's head, as if he were trying to kill him with granite chips.

When Rocklin's rifle was fully reloaded, he let Heller fire his third shot, then unloaded on him, and ducked. Heller didn't fire again. Rocklin waited a full minute—and another full minute. He wondered where the soldiers were, and the special agents Bannister had sent. The town below seemed very quiet.

Rocklin waited another two minutes and decided to move. It was a calculated risk; Heller might just stand up behind his rock and shoot him. On the other hand, if Heller knew that if each man waited for the other to show himself they could be here all week; and time, and any soldiers below, would be on Rocklin's side. Also, and this was the main thing, Heller had acted like a man who was headed somewhere. The longer Rocklin stayed put, the better chance the outlaw leader had of getting where he was going.

Rocklin led Buck swiftly down the trail until he came to the spot where Heller had holed up. He wasn't dead. He wasn't sitting bleeding. He just wasn't there. There was only a horse, standing alone.

Rocklin climbed the shoulder of rock that hid the trail from the town below and looked around. Four feet away, hanging from a projecting rock above, was a rope. At the bottom end of the rope was another trail, so narrow as to be almost nonexistent. It was slanting down the opposite way and was completely unconnected with the main trail. And at the bottom of it, struggling along a sloping stretch of mud, was Heller. He was carrying an old suitcase over his shoulder on a rope sling.

He seemed to be heading for a miserable-looking shack at the opposite edge of the muddy slope, and every once in a while he would glance at his back trail. Rocklin crouched, waited for Heller's latest glance, and immediately afterward jumped for the rope. He slid down in a hurry, knowing that if Heller glanced back and saw him, he would be picked off like an overgrown raccoon. He made it, then took cover to watch Heller.

Heller was headed for the shack. He whistled twice, then twice more. A door at the back of the shack opened and a woman peered out into the night. Heller said something to her that Rocklin couldn't catch, and she opened the door and motioned him on.

He was wading through the last of the mudbanks when the door opened wide and a man came out. He had a shotgun, and he unloaded both barrels at Heller. Heller staggered, but he didn't stop. He palmed his Colt and lurched forward, firing all the time. The man in the doorway brought out his six-shooter and fired repeatedly as Heller went down. Heller was flat on his face in the mud.

When Rocklin reached the scene, the woman had the suitcase open and was staring down at the money.

"The dirty pig," she said. "He kept me half-starved and half-froze to death down in this filthy shack." She was in her nightclothes, and her tangled red hair, although real, looked like a moth-eaten wig.

Rocklin went to see about the man in the doorway. It was Big Jim Haggard. "He got me in the right hip, and just below my right armpit," he said. "I'll live."

People were showing up. They were sleepy, and looked as if they had dressed in a hurry. The town had not been deserted, it had been asleep for the first time in over a week.

"Is there a doctor?" Rocklin asked the small crowd. Some of the people were recognizing the owner of the town where they lived and worked. "There's no doctor," one man said. "There's a man who patches us up until we can get into Russell Junction. I'll get him."

The woman with the tangled red hair screamed. Rocklin whirled and saw Dain Heller raising himself to one knee in the mud and pointing his six-shooter. He was aiming at Jim Haggard, who was half sitting, half lying in a patch of eerie light from the doorway. Rocklin slipped the .38 from under his arm and shot Heller three times.

"Good, good!" the redhead screamed. "Shoot him again! Filthy pig! He let other men take their whores up there, and even their kids. And they weren't even married! And look at me! Look at *me!*"

Rocklin was feeling dizzy. The shock was so great, he thought he was going to black out. The women and kids! Where was his mind! Those faces at the doors; that boy being jerked inside. He had forgotten, completely forgotten! He turned and staggered through the mud slope toward the rocky path upward. He wasn't sure he was going to make it. He took gasping breaths and kept going.

The women and kids! Clancey didn't know

about them because Rocklin forgot to tell him. What if one of them fired at the troops? And he had sought to dynamite both trails and starve everybody.

He kept lashing himself mentally, and it helped get him up the rope and into his saddle. Buck had rested some, but it had been a hard trip for him, too. When they reached the top of the mesa, Rocklin said, "I'm sorry, fella, but we have to run. Go!"

It was about seven miles, and Rocklin had to pull Buck back every mile or so and let him walk and blow.

The town was so quiet he could hear the pop of coals as the fires fizzled out. He thought he was too late. He could see shadows, a few figures moving around in the flickering light. They seemed very silent. It was too late!

The figures emerged from weird light; they looked as though they were dancing. The strange dizzy spell was broken when Rocklin heard what sounded like the cocking of twenty Springfield Army rifles.

Somebody said, "Halt. Who goes there? And you better have the right answer, mister."

"I'm the crazy miner," Rocklin said. "Point the guns somewhere else. Where's Sergeant Clancey?"

A corporal that Rocklin had seen before stepped forward. "He's at the fourth house over. Some of them are holed up there, and he's about to blast them out."

The troopers were in a half circle around the house, aiming their guns. "Clancey! Hold it!"

Rocklin shouted. "Don't shoot!"

The sergeant turned and stared at Rocklin. "You again. Did you get the man you were after?"

"Yes. There are women and children in there."

"Someone fired a couple of shots!"

"Could be a frightened woman. Or even a kid. Let me talk to them."

"Port arms! Don't shoot unless I say so. Got it?" he told his men. "Go ahead," he said to Rocklin.

Rocklin cupped his hands to his mouth and called out toward the house. "Heller sent me to tell you to give up. You'll be safe. The troopers won't hurt you."

"Where are our men?" a tremulous female voice called.

"Dead or arrested," Rocklin said. "They don't want anything to happen to you. Come out."

"Who are you?" the woman called. "I can't recall ever seeing you before."

"I've never been up here. I was the boss's contact in Rand. He got out."

"I don't believe you."

"What does that matter? What are you going to do, stay in there forever? I promise you that you won't be hurt. Bring the children and come out."

There were only four women and five children in the house. As they filed out, the troopers brought their rifles down to order arms without being told. The women and children were ragged and unkempt. They looked scared and cold and hungry. Some of the troopers were swearing bitterly from the depth of their feeling and their exhaustion.

"Shut up!" Clancey ordered. "Get these people down to the camp and feed them." The men couldn't believe what they were seeing. They weren't moving, they were just staring. "Move!" Clancey bellowed in his fiercest parade-ground voice. Then he turned to Rocklin and said savagely, "What in the hell kept you?"

Twenty-Four

Rocklin woke up in the infirmary at Fort Hatcher. The surgeon, Major Cox, was looking down at him.

"Good," the major said. "I was wondering when you were going to wake up."

"How long have I been asleep?" Rocklin asked.

"Two days and two nights. Now don't try to jump out of bed like that! I want you to stay down for a couple more days. Did you feel any dizziness when you raised up like that?"

"No."

"All right. Sit up slowly. I'm going to hold a lamp right up to your eyes, first one and then the other, to see how your pupils react."

"My pupils?"

"They'll close by themselves against the light. I'm trying to see if there could be any kind of pressure on your brain. I'll be testing the movement and feeling in your hands and feet, too. Just try to relax."

"Well?" Rocklin asked when Cox had finished.

"You seem to be in good shape. Move around a little if you want to, but if you feel any dizziness at all, or if you think you are going to black out, lie down. Are you hungry?"

"Yes."

"Good. You can eat anything you want. If we have it."

What they had was beef and potatoes. Rocklin enjoyed them, then he went to sleep and hardly stirred for another twenty-four hours.

This time when he woke up it was Riddle who was standing over him. "Ah, you've rejoined us. How are you feeling?" he asked.

"I'll tell you in a minute." Rocklin sat up easily. "How are you?"

"Fine. They have a good surgeon here."

"You wouldn't happen to know about my horse?"

"There are dozens of experts on horses around here," Riddle said. "I'm sure he's being well taken care of. I saw the reunion of the Legrande family. I thought you'd like to know."

"Good. How do you get some coffee and a few dozen flapjacks in this place?"

"I'll show you. The family is still here."

"What? Why?"

"The young lady had a slight relapse. She's all right though," Riddle added quickly. "It's the post that isn't all right. She has set it on its ear."

"I can believe that," Rocklin said. "I don't want

them to know I'm here."

"They may already know. I'm not sure about that."

Colonal Race and Major Cox came in. "I heard you were awake," Cox said. "How are you feeling?"

"Fine. I was asking Riddle where I could get some coffee and flapjacks."

"I'd be grateful if you'd eat with me in my quarters," Race said. "You too Riddle. Is it all right, Major?"

"No reason why not," Cox said.

"Ah. Yes," Riddle said. "Uh, I have a sort of previous engagement, Colonel, if it's all right with you."

The colonel smiled. "Of course. I don't blame you."

"I would just as soon not encounter the Legrande family," Rocklin said.

"You won't," Race said. "They don't know you're here, as far as I know. Of course, everybody usually knows everything in a place like this. But your name isn't generally known—if it is your name."

Rocklin was treated royally, and after breakfast—lunch for the colonel—was over and they had settled back, Race took a wire from his pocket and handed it to Rocklin. "This came about an hour after I had left for Rand," he said.

The wire was from Bannister. It read: HIGHEST POLITICAL SOURCE SAYS UNDER NO CIR-CUMSTANCES REPEAT UNDER NO CIR-

CUMSTANCES ARE ESCAPE ROUTES TO BE DYNAMITED.

Rocklin said, "I would laugh if I was sure you weren't in serious trouble."

Race smiled. He took out another wire and handed it to Rocklin. It was from the War Department. It read: REQUEST IMMEDIATE EXPLANATION OF DYNAMITING IN RAND.

Rocklin gazed at Race's expressionless face. "And?" he asked.

The colonel shrugged. "I told them I was already on my way to Rand when your man's wire arrived. And I was following direct orders to cooperate fully with you."

"Is that it? Have you heard anything more?"

"Not a whisper. I won't, since the Heller gang has been wiped out so efficiently."

"Good."

Race eyed Rocklin. "Tell me, Rocklin. When you suggested the dynamite, did you know there were women and children up there?"

"Yes."

"Yes?" Race was staring at Rocklin.

"I forgot," Rocklin said, meeting the colonel's stare.

Race continued to stare, but his gaze slowly shifted to distant times and places. He cleared his throat. "Yes. Well. It can happen in a war. The thing is to not let it prey on your mind."

"Where are they now?" Rocklin asked.

"Here. Being fed and clothed. The men, and some of the officers' wives, have taken them under their wing, so to speak. I suppose the youngsters will eventually become wards of the court. I don't know what will happen to the women."

The colonel brooded for a moment, then remembered his role as a host and became more expansive. "I tell you, the post has been turned upside down. Riddle's basking in universal approval, and the Legrandes are the toast of the whole area." He hesitated, then said, "Haggard has called."

"Recovering, is he?"

"Doing well. His wounds weren't too bad. He said he'd been watching that house for two days. Of course, it's his town."

Rocklin didn't pursue the subject, and Race suppressed his curiosity like a gentleman. "How many men did you lose?" Rocklin asked.

"Four to the river, and three to the Heller bunch. It probably would have been a lot more, but for you."

"And you. The dynamiting was most timely. Are the towns still there?"

"Yes, mostly. The engineers did a remarkable job. By the way, Clancey looked in on you three or four times while you were sleeping. He said the last thing he did before you blacked out was yell at you. I think he wants to recruit you."

Rocklin laughed. "I could do worse," he said. "Where can I find him?"

"You can't. He'll be out for a week on patrol. But you may stay as long as you want to, you know."

"I'll be leaving as soon as I send a wire, if I may

impose on you again."

"The place is yours."

Rocklin's telegram to Bannister said: PLEASE GET WIRE OFF IMMEDIATELY AND TELL M I AM FINE AND LETTER FOLLOWS. R.

Bannister had phoned Rocklin's wife two days earlier.

Twenty-Five

Mary Tillman
17 Washington Square Place
New York City, New York

My beloved wife,

Forgive the delay, but I have been using a minor wound as an excuse to sleep and otherwise loaf for a few days. I had a gash in my scalp, but the hair will cover it, and you won't even be able to see it by the time I get home. In the meantime, I hope you haven't believed anything you read in the newspapers.

I have seen a few of them, and I wonder how anyone ever finds out anything for sure by reading them. This is the fourth time—or maybe the fifth—I have been directly involved in an event that has been reported in the newspapers, and there have always been inaccuracies, and even misinformation in the accounts. It makes a man wonder. I was relieved to discover that my name was mentioned only once, and that in a local paper. It came out Brockland, and I am glad of that, at least.

I am in Russell Junction, and I will catch a train tomorrow and come directly home. Trains have been delayed while a crew repairs a washout down the line. But you have probably read about that, haven't you? It seems that, as bad as they are, newspapers are useful.

Are you and the children well? I can't get you off my mind. Maybe now is the time for that trip.

A peculiar thing happened to me today. A young man (He was a puerile youth, actually) came to my hotel room and offered me money for my story of the kidnapping and rescue of the Legrande children. He seemed very sure that I had some kind of private and personal information, although he was careful not to say just what the information was or where he got it. I couldn't guess his source, and I am not sure I want to. He didn't once use my name.

He knew a great deal that he could have learned only from someone directly involved, though, and he had a very excited—I would say agitated—manner, as if taking part in some kind of desperate intrigue.

I feel sure that the *world,* borrowing a bit of his hyperbole, will soon be favored with a lurid tale about the whole "Heller-Legrande Affair." No doubt there will be some implied link between the notorious outlaw leader and the famous millionaire sportsman. Once he has the basic structure in place, he can go as high as he wants with his

Babelian tower of fiction.

I finally had to throw him out.

If the incident had occurred in New York City it probably wouldn't have seemed so peculiar. But in Russell Junction? It struck me as another example of the increasingly bizarre mixture of the real and the phony that constitutes "getting ahead" in America today, and I wonder what's down the road for us.

I made a bad mistake this trip, and it was only luck that innocent people did not die as a result. Maybe I have outworn my usefulness.

That sounds suspiciously like an appeal for sympathy, doesn't it? Well, it won't take forever for the train to get here. It only seems so.

You have probably read numerous articles about the Legrandes. It is an unusual family. I'll tell you all about them when I get home.

Until then
I remain
Your loving husband,
William R. Tillman

Twenty-Six

Riddle came to see Rocklin in his hotel room. The knock on the door surprised Rocklin, and the thought occurred to him that he ought to move to the other hotel in town until his train came.

He was glad to see Riddle though. The man had made an impression on him.

"I wouldn't know you," Riddle said. "You merge into your background like a chameleon, don't you?"

"How did you find me, then?" Rocklin asked.

"Oh, I inquired around. Carefully, of course," he quickly added. "No names were used. This isn't a very big place, you know."

"I'm glad you did."

"I'm getting most of the credit, you know," Riddle said. "My name has been in three eastern papers." He shrugged ruefully. "Spelled three different ways, and none of them correct, mind you. You know there is no way I can set the record straight without compromising you."

"And you've made a hit with Miss Legrande," Rocklin said. "Congratulations."

"Oh, you've heard about that."

"Who hasn't?"

"Yes. Well, that part has been exaggerated by the reporters. You can't do much about that. The real news is that I've been summoned to Chicago. The president of the railroad wants to see me. What about that!"

"Congratulations again."

"I've heard talk . . . Well, remember when we talked about gossip among special agents?"

"When *you* talked about it."

"Yes. You were going to shoot me, weren't you?"

"Not fatally."

Riddle laughed. "Well, anyway . . . You're practically a legend, you know. I didn't believe you really existed until . . . Look, Rocklin, I've heard, from strictly private sources, I mean, that you know a lot of people. I mean really big people. You wouldn't happen to know the president of the railroad, would you? I mean, the story is that you can get things done when nobody else can."

Rocklin laughed. He wasn't sure he felt like laughing, but he was trying to give Riddle the benefit of the doubt. "You're believing stories now? And I thought you had the makings of a pretty good troubleshooter."

Riddle didn't take the hint. He had glimpsed the golden ladder and was hell-bent for it. "I'm serious, Rocklin. Do you have any influence with anyone in Chicago? I need all the help I can get."

Rocklin wasn't sure he had any reason to be slightly depressed. Riddle was an excellent man, and he was certainly there when needed. He had intelligence, great courage, and even a certain flair.

It was nothing but a difference in attitudes. Perhaps a difference between generations.

But he did wonder if the young man's outstanding qualities would, as time went on, survive in competition with driving ambition.

"I'll write a good letter," he said. "Tell me where to send it."

"That's great, sir! I can't tell you how grateful I am. And I can't tell you what a privilege it's been working with you."

"And don't worry, I'll get your name right," Rocklin joked.

Riddle didn't stay long after he had written his name and address for Rocklin. He was too excited. Rocklin wasn't sorry to see him go.

Rocklin took a walk. Russell Junction was the same, only more so. People were everywhere, busy people who lived and worked in the town, and eager curiosity seekers who had drifted in from all directions. Prices had tripled and quadrupled, and there were hawkers of souvenirs—what the relics might be or where they came from Rocklin couldn't imagine—and "guides" promising exciting tours of Rand and Pine Hollow and the waterfall trail.

The town was living high on the hog. It was

well situated, and there was a river a few miles below it that ran through the prairies and deserts of three states. It had escaped any major storm damage.

The atmosphere, so washed and sparkling clear that it almost hurt a person's eyes, was full of tension and energy. People were making and spending money. It was exhilarating.

Rocklin walked around the town, and out of town, for two hours. Then he took Buck for a run in the still soggy meadow below it. It didn't make Buck any more willing to get on a train, but Rocklin managed that, too, with the help of plenty of sugar.

The station agent announced that the line was open and the train would be leaving in half an hour. Rocklin went back to his hotel, changed clothes, and headed for the station.

There was a festive mood up and down the station platform. Rocklin felt more of his tension draining away as he breathed the thin and heady air.

The Legrande family was coming toward him down the narrow platform. He faded into the environment. John Claude Legrande was busy herding the family toward the private car, just behind the baggage and mail car where Buck was.

But Rose Legrande caught Rocklin's eye. She started visibly and her cheeks turned pink. She was going to stop and say something, but people, reporters and other sensation mongers, were dogging the family. Rocklin shook his head, and

Rose Legrande passed by without apparent recognition.

Priscilla Legrande tugged at her mother's sleeve and said, "Mother, did you see that man? It was Mr. Rocklin."

"Of course I didn't see Mr. Rocklin. Be quiet, child."

"Mr. Rocklin?" Dick asked. "Where, where?"

"Mother, I am not a child, and I know it was Mr. Rocklin."

"Priscilla, please! This is not the time."

Dick was trying to head back through the crowd. He was jumping up and down, trying to see down the platform. "Mr. Rocklin!" he shouted.

The reporters pounced. "Who? Who? What did you say?" one of them asked. "Who's Mr. Conklin?"

"What's going on?" Legrande asked. "We have to board the train."

Dick was quick. "Nothing. Nothing, Dad."

"It was Mr. Rocklin," his wife told him in a soft voice.

"I saw him too," Priscilla said.

Legrande had had some experience with the press, and he knew better than to tell them anything important, or anything at all that could be garbled in a way that could hurt or embarrass anyone.

"Get on the train," he urged his family. "Hurry. Hurry, now."

Other reporters picked up the Conklin name. "Mr. Legrande, who's Conklin?" one of them yelled as the Legrandes disappeared into the private car.

"May I sit down, Mr. Rocklin?"

It was a day later, and Rocklin was in the dining car studying the rather astonishing menu—fresh strawberries and cream were among the more ordinary items offered for dessert. He looked up and saw Rose Legrande.

She had changed clothes, wore no hat, and had put on glasses, trying her best to be nondescript. Among the concepts she had learned as a child was, "A fool's name and a fool's face are always seen in a public place." She had walked through the train past reporters.

Rocklin concealed his astonishment. He half rose and said, "Please do."

She didn't waste words. "I have come to invite you to dinner in our car," she said. "Everyone is most eager to see you."

Rocklin hesitated. He didn't enjoy trying to cope with gratitude after a job of work. But she could have sent her husband. She could have sent a note by the conductor.

"Mrs. Legrande," he said. "I . . . It's not necessary . . ."

She interrupted, something she never did. "Mr. Rocklin, if a simple gesture of gratitude is to be effective, there must be a recipient who is . . . *civilized* enough to accept it gracefully."